CW01559079

SHADOW OF THE WICKED

A THREE KINGDOMS NOVELLA

DOUGLAS W.T. SMITH

Copyright © 2021 Douglas W.T. Smith All rights reserved

The characters and events portrayed in this book are fictitious. Any similarity to real persons, living or dead, is coincidental and not intended by the author.
No part of this book may be reproduced, or stored in a retrieval system, or transmitted in any form or by any means, electronic, mechanical, photocopying, recording, or otherwise, without express written permission of the publisher.

ISBN-13: 9798737270797

Cover design by: MiblArt
Map Art by: MiauArt
Library of Congress Control Number: 2018675309
Printed in the United States of America

ACKNOWLEDGMENTS

I want to thank all my beta readers for taking the time and making the effort to not just read my draft book but send detailed comments and feedback. This book is far better thanks to you.

I personally want to thank my wife. She was the one who had to put up with me. That she did with love, patience, and encouragement instead of strangling me. She is my best friend. Every day, even if we have had an argument, I am genuinely amazed I get to spend my life with her. I try to let her know how much I appreciate her, as often as I can. This is me letting you know, too.

You have this book because of her.

"The bond of brothers is stronger than any forged metal in the world. Bound together by blood and nothing can break it."

JAROMIR

The fireplace crackled and radiated an ominous ambience in the room. Jaromir's closest comrades sat at the round table in front of him. He stood over a map of the Three Kingdoms with a candle in his hand, shadows danced across the parchment from the flickering flame, and three pints of ale weighed it down around the edge.

"I need a message delivered." Jaromir stared at his comrades.

Shaydin and Kadir sat next to him, glancing at the map.

"Is that why you called us over here?" Shaydin asked, his husky voice tried to whisper, in case anyone was listening outside Jaromir's home. His long brown hair tied into a topknot, and the leather armor reflected the obscure oranges and yellows from the candles in the room.

Jaromir nodded, brushing his wispy hair off his face.

"I thought you looked paler than you usually do," Kadir commented, grabbing his pint, and taking a sip out of it. The froth hung to his short beard, imitating his curly blonde hair. "Where does it need to be taken?"

"Does Talmage know?" Kadir leaned over the table.

Jaromir shook his head. "I can't trust him."

"He's your twin. You can trust him," Shaydin assured him.

Jaromir placed the candle on the table and cleared his throat.

He looked over his shoulders down the hallway to see if his wife could hear him. She was out of earshot. "You know we haven't spoken for years. I don't know who he could tell."

"Then there's your answer." Shaydin grabbed his pint, his hand enclosed by a gauntlet. "If it's too important for anyone else to know, you can't trust us either. We don't mind telling a few tales after a few of these." He winked at Jaromir and took a sip.

"I know you two won't tell the wrong person." Jaromir glanced at the other comrade. "I can trust both of you. Kadir, you've saved my life countless times from our enemy and what has Tal done for me?"

"It's not that I've forgotten who saved whose life, but I feel caught between you and Talmage," Kadir admitted. "He needs to be a part of our order, or I'm not your messenger bird anymore." He took a sip from his ale and wiped the froth of his beard. "You call it Brother-in-Arms, but *where* is your brother?"

Shaydin stepped around Kadir and grabbed Jaromir's shoulder. "Don't listen to him. We'll fight by each other's sides until the day we die, whether we're killed by delivering messages or wicked sorcerers." He faced Kadir. "It's what we signed up for when he asked us, all those years ago. Kadir, you wouldn't be here if it wasn't for Jaromir." Shaydin glared at him. "So, shut your mouth and let him speak."

"Keep it down. Zylah could be listening to us." Jaromir hushed him. "This message needs to be delivered at haste."

Shaydin and Kadir looked at each other.

"You can trust us," Shaydin said.

Kadir sighed and nodded. "When do you want us to leave?"

"I'll meet you in two days' time in Tarnsby, but you need to leave at first light," Jaromir smirked.

A cold breeze slammed the front door. Jaromir glanced at it, lifting his head from the round table. He had been staring at the map since his comrades left. Jaromir studied the villages and wondered if his plan to cross The Cleave unnoticed and reach the other kingdoms would come to fruition. He left the dining room and crept to the front door.

"It's just the wind." His wife appeared. Her curly reddish-brown hair swayed behind her. She opened it and looked out the front of their home. "See, there's nothing."

"What do you think you're doing?" Jaromir rushed and slammed the door shut. "You don't know what or who is out there."

"What could be out there?" she asked, narrowing her dark eyes at him.

"There are things you couldn't imagine." Jaromir inflated his chest, returning a deep glare with his icy blue eyes.

"We live in the inner wall of Valenor. Nothing like that would ever happen here. Kadir or Shaydin must've left it open."

Jaromir rubbed his wispy beard. "Possibly, but sorcerers and shapeshifters could easily sneak in the shadows. It's only a matter of time before they do and before *he* does."

"Who's he?" Zylah asked with a high-pitched voice.

Jaromir rubbed the purple scar stretching down his arm. "You know who I'm talking about. The person that killed my parents and gave me this scar."

Zylah placed her hand on his shoulder as he his sleeve, staring at the scar in the candlelight. "Did you know you share that same scar with Talmage?"

"Unfortunately, it's one of the things we share."

"You know, Pius will never come for us," said Zylah, letting of his shoulder.

"He's out there, and no one will be safe until he's dead." Jaromir walked back into the room and picked up the candle.

"We're safe now."

For now. Jaromir thought as she disappeared out of his sight. He hovered the flickering light over the west coast of Valenor and lowered it onto Tarnsby. A red cross marked over it, as several other places had across Esterford.

Jaromir let out a deep sigh and lifted his head. Before him and above the fireplace, an ancient sword glistened in the flickering light. It was passed down from the emperor, and it watched over the dining space. He had received it for his years of honorary duty as the Knight Commander of the Empire Order, and none of his family were there for him. He clenched his fist and faced his wife. Her long curly hair hung in front of her as she entered and studied the map. Her tawny brown skin sparkled as if she had just bathed.

Zylah entered the room. "Have you heard from Talmage?"

"No, I haven't." Jaromir resumed looking at the map spread across the table.

She thumped her hand onto the map. "Have you tried to contact him?"

Jaromir shook his head and cleared his throat.

"Why not?"

He straightened his back and glanced at his wife. He stood a foot taller than her and doubled her width. "Don't act surprised."

"When did you last speak to him?" She inflated her chest.

Jaromir embraced another argument. Now that his guests were gone, the truth of their relationship would resume. "I don't know," he snapped back.

"Every time you invite your companions over, you never invite your brother," her voice grew louder. Her veins throbbed in her neck and her eyes narrowed in the soft light. "When *was* the last time you spoke to him?" she demanded him to answer.

His lips were dry. "I need a drink," Jaromir muttered.

"You gave up on that, just like your brother," Zylah inflated her chest and defended Talmage.

"You don't know how hard it is to not drink when you're pestering me." Jaromir dismissed her comments.

"Then answer the question!"

"It was at Agustin's burial."

"That was two years ago!"

"I tried to contact him after it." Jaromir couldn't contain his anger. "He never returned any of my letters. Before that, he'd become someone other than my brother. I couldn't be around him anymore. If anything, I made the greatest choice to stay out of his life. Our young brotherly bond faded with our age."

Zylah took deep breaths and closed her eyes. Finally, she said with a calm tone. "Did you know Bethany took her life?"

"Who told you that?" Jaromir asked, his mood instantly shifted.

"Talmage." Zylah turned and left the room.

Questions rushed through his thoughts. He wanted to ask all of them at the same time. Had she been talking to him? Where did she see him? But instead, he chased after her and grabbed her shoulder. "Why didn't you tell me this?"

"You don't care about anyone but yourself!"

"When did this happen?"

"Two months ago," Zylah said, shrugging his hand off her.

"I'm going to find him." A sense of urgency ran through Jaromir to find his brother.

It was true, he hadn't spoken to his brother for years, but he felt guilty and ashamed for not being there for him when his wife died. *Maybe something happened to her.* As he grabbed his sword and slid on his armor, he remembered Bethany wasn't at Agustin's burial. A more profound feeling of remorse and shame pressed on him as he concealed his body with a long woolen cloak.

"You haven't cared about him, and now all of a sudden you chose to find him?" Zylah chased after him.

"You wouldn't understand," Jaromir muttered.

"Do you think he'll forgive you?"

Jaromir stopped. *After all this time we've been apart, would he forget our quarrels?*

"You don't know where he is." Zylah rushed to the door and stood before him, blocking his way.

"I have a faint clue where he'll be." *I know where I'd be if I didn't give up drinking.*

"You can't just leave me here alone. What about the sorcerers and shapeshifters, like you said?"

Jaromir adjusted the cloak over his head. "If someone comes here, use the sword above the fireplace, but you should be safe. We live in the inner wall. Nothing like that will ever happen." He smirked at her and ran outside.

The thick rain droplets thud onto his cloak. He ran across the puddled stone path. The street was empty, and the night was loud. He turned and saw Zylah standing at the front door of their home. Candlelight's flickered on the window of the second level. She must have left one up there, but he didn't remember her going upstairs all night. He shrugged the thought and made haste for his brother. The stacked houses clasped the shadows, hiding the contents of the narrow alleyways. Jaromir held the pommel of his sword. An icy shiver ran down his spine. He could feel people watching him from between the buildings. He picked up his pace. *There's only one place Tal would be.* He distracted the unknown with his task. He had always put his tasks and objectives above all. In his line of work, he knew emotions could never hinder his goal.

It was one of the rules of his order. *Never let emotions cloud your sense of judgment.*

Jaromir peered out of the corner of his eye. He caught a glance of a boot tuck in the shadow of a wall as a flash of lightning lit the sky. Jaromir ran in the downpour. Gusts of wind swirled in the streets as he paced down the cobbled stone roads. The taste of fresh cool water filtered from his hood as he came around the street corner to face The Amalgamate. A tavern that linked through the city wall. He spun around, and three cloak figures stood before him.

"If you can't be stealth in this weather, you'll be more useful dead." The cloaked man that stood in the middle held out his hand.

Sparks of lightning shot out from his fist. Flying past Jaromir's cheek, slicing it open. Steam rose in the crispy night from his wound.

"Things are more interesting now. I don't think you know who I am." Jaromir smiled at them, even though they wouldn't be able to see his facial features. "I am a man that has been eliminating magick users, like you three, for a very long time. I am the night's shadows that'll make sure the new day will be welcomed with a bright light. Our world will be a better place, once you're gone."

The tallest dark figure stepped forward. "You're missing something, old man." His shrill voice whispered in the rain.

"What's that, you vile piece of shit?"

"There are six of us."

Jaromir's heart dropped. He spun around and caught a glance of an iron staff smacking him to the ground. After all his years of studying and training, his heightened senses had failed him. His vision faded as black boots splashed in the puddles closer to him.

The blurred face crept down in front of his. "We finally meet, Jaromir."

TALMAGE

"Water?" A harsh voice asked, casting a shadow over Talmage.

He lifted his head and opened his weary eyes. A broad man with thick hairy arms leaned on the bar, blocking the light from the tavern.

The man slid the pint of water to Talmage. He accepted with a grunt. His hand shook the glass as he sipped the cool liquid, soothing his parched throat.

"Thank you, but an ale would have sufficed, Haggith." Talmage grinned.

"You've had your belly full for tonight. Finish that and head on home."

Talmage gulped the water and slammed the glass on the wooden table. "I'll see you tomorrow." He stood from the stool and stumbled towards the door.

"This won't fix your problems."

"I know it doesn't fix it, Haggith, but it eases my pain."

Talmage staggered out of the Amalgamate tavern. The clouds above rumbled as if they were furious at him. He hadn't seen his brother after Agustin was murdered, and his wife had taken her own life. Whenever someone came close to him or he began to love, they would disappear.

After Agustin died, Jaromir never returned his messages. He visited their homestead numerous times, and Zylah said he was out, but Talmage saw his brother peering from one of the windows in their manor.

One fateful night another sorcerer had invited Talmage to reside with him. He continued his magick training, and the sorcerer showed him everything, putting him through tormenting trials of relentless and exhausting lessons. The sorcerer took Talmage under his wing, but as he mulled over his haunting past with pints of ale, every night, Talmage believed magick had cost him his wife, Bethany. He had kept it all a secret and told her he had been training with his brother.

Maybe she found out I was a sorcerer, and that's why she took her own life. The same dreadful thought repeated in his mind every night.

A flash of lightning disturbed his thoughts. For that moment, the disheveled homes and broken streets blazed in the divine light before it was swallowed by the night.

Talmage swayed along the building wall, using his hands to guide him. He glanced around to see if anyone was near him. After his drunken judgment, he muttered to himself. "Ardeat ignis."

A small flame conjured in his hand. The dancing flames comforted him, warming his empty and restless soul. After all that had happened, magick had been the constant and stable thing in his harrowing life.

"Didn't I teach you to keep it a secret?" A wispy voice crept from an alleyway.

Talmage flicked his wrist, and the flame extinguished. His eyes adjusted to the figure before him. "You scared me, Pius."

"What if I was one of the guards or worse, your brother?"

Talmage staggered towards him. "My brother would never stand up to me."

"Don't be so confident. You're lucky it was only me otherwise, all that I've trained you for would have been for naught." Pius stood beside him.

Talmage felt his judging gaze scan over him. "Do you pity me?"

"I do not pity you. I hope you believe me when I say this, but your time as the next Sorcerer Monarch is in fruition with one last piece to move into position."

Talmage stopped and leered at him.

Pius' black messy hair concealed the wrinkles on his face. Under his hooded cloak, he wore his custom armor and a dagger on his waist. Another deep rumble in the disappointing clouds filled the ominous sky.

Talmage swallowed his fears. "Do you plan on killing me?"

Pius' thin grin stretched across his face. "I don't plan on killing you, Talmage. I wouldn't have exhausted my skills to train you. No, that would've been a waste of time on both our behalf's." He glanced down at his dagger. "I can never be sure when I need protection in the city turmoil. I have many followers but even more enemies." He tightened his hood around his neck.

"Then what is the last piece of your grand plan?"

"Your final test. Come with me." Pius gripped his arm and dragged him into the alleyway.

Talmage narrowed his eyes at the buildings. His head swayed from the gallons of ale he consumed prior. He withdrew his hand from Pius' long thin fingers. "Where are we going?"

"We're almost here. Come." He paced and urged Talmage deeper into the bending and tapering alleyway.

After a while, the pair of sorcerers emerged from the thin gap between the buildings and stood in front of a house. Under the moonlight, Talmage squinted with curiosity at the strange place. It had vines and trees choking the side and roof. It stretched into the darkness, and a great light flashed from a window gap.

"What was that?" Talmage swayed.

"The Blacksmith."

"Why are we here?"

Pius reached into his cloak and pulled out a small potion bottle. "Have this. It'll help clear your mind from all that stinking ale."

Talmage hesitantly received it. As he grabbed it, he studied the black smear on his palm from magick. He wiped it on his cloak. "Will this poison me?"

"It won't poison you, Talmage. Like I said, it'll clear your mind and ready you for your final trial."

"Are you going to tell me what it is?"

"Drink, and I will." He smirked.

Talmage peered at him before he gulped the small liquid. The honey and a bitter lemon taste swirled in his mouth. He tapped the last drops of the bottle onto his tongue.

"I'm glad you enjoyed it. That'll be the last thing you have until you make it out." Pius laughed. His wicked and sneering cackle pierced the calm thin air.

With a flash of panic, Talmage shoved his fingers down this throat. Pius clicked his fingers, and two large brutes appeared from behind him and grabbed his arms.

"Morten and Renold. Put him into place. The last piece is ready for our dominion."

Talmage kicked and thrust his body, but the men held him back. "This isn't worth it, Pius. Morten. Renold. Don't listen to him."

"Don't disobey me, or it'll be the last thing you do." Pius lifted his hand to threaten his servants. The two brutes gripped harder around Talmage's arm. "Trust me, Talmage, this will all be worth it." His malicious laugh echoed in the alleyway.

Talmage felt his arms weakened, and his eyes grew heavy. He needed to scream for help and break free, but he couldn't stay awake any longer. His neck flopped forward.

My brother could never stand up to me. His words faded into a chasm of darkness.

JAROMIR

Blood filled Jaromir's mouth. He wiggled his head and opened his eyes. Crusty discharge stuck to his eyelashes and blurred his vision from a hazy glow. Thin shadows crept along the floor like demons. Jaromir licked his lips and swallowed the blood.

Where am I? Jaromir caught an odor of hot iron. His hips throbbed, and his temples shot piercing streaks across his forehead.

He scanned the surrounding darkness and lifted his hands to wipe his face, but iron shackles restricted his wrists. He squinted at his bare chest and breeches. Above him, a network of chains extended to the ceiling, and as he squirmed, rough wood scratched his back.

Jaromir's heart raced, and his breath grew fast and shallow. He peered into the darkness surrounding him. He was chained to a table in the middle of a room. It seemed small enough for a tiny cellar underneath a tavern, but there were no barrels of wine or ale near him, only faint shadows, and obscure objects softly gleaming upon the wall. The room had a stone door, no windows or openings, a high ceiling with chains suspended from it. In the corner, a stone well sat with vines running up the wall.

Jaromir kicked his ankles and pulled at his arms. His chest tightened, and panic shivered through his limbs. The dark glistening walls felt as if they were closing in. A high-pitched ringing noise of a hammer smacking on an anvil rung in his ears, and gushing flames of burning iron radiated under the door.

"Let me out!" He shouted.

No one came to his aid. *Those filthy sorcerers.* He winced and scrunched his face. "Dammit!" He thrust his arms, flailing like a fish out of water. The coarse table scraping his back as he gasped for air.

The stone door swung open, and a thickly built figure stood in the doorway.

Jaromir squinted at the person moving closer. With each step, he shook the ground.

"Who are you? Unchain me!" Jaromir demanded.

As the person approached, Jaromir noticed the large man shared similar features to a troll with wide arms, thick legs like tree trunks, and a hairless body.

The man remained silent as he walked to the wall, leaving the door open. Outside, a dark corridor stone stretched into the darkness.

"Hey, hey!" Jaromir tried to get his attention with a gentle voice. The man twisted his broad neck and shoulders towards him. "Come on. You can let me out. I won't tell anyone about this, okay?"

The man grunted and returned to his task in the corner. He lifted the lid for the well and slid it on.

"You fat piece of shit! Let me out!"

He grunted at Jaromir's remark and paced over to the other corner of the room. As Jaromir readied his chest for an onslaught of verbal abuse, another figure appeared in the doorway. The hooded person stood silently, watching, and leaning on his staff. His robe floated behind him like a banner flapping in the wind.

Jaromir squinted at the man. "Who is it?" He peered in the darkness.

"I wasn't gone all that long, my dear friend." His voice was deep and hollow, as if he spoke in an empty hall.

The man stepped closer. His wrinkled face came clear in the feeble light and his eyes narrowed at Jaromir. Under his loose robe, a chest-plate shimmered like a wet stone, and a dagger hung on his waist.

Jaromir recognized the face. "YOU!" He felt his heart thudding in his chest, and his breathing deepened. "Untie me!" He propelled his arms towards him, arching his back and wriggling his shoulders.

"That's quite unfortunate." The robed man gestured the other man to close the door.

"Let me out of here, you filthy sorcerer!"

The table beneath Jaromir trembled with each step of the brute as he moved from the corner to shut the door. From the faint shade of gray in the hallway, Jaromir's vision was gone, but he could hear the large man moving closer to him, and an eerie feeling tingled his fingertips.

"Where are you? Show yourself!" Jaromir ordered.

Blind in the dark, Jaromir heard the hooded man shift like a cat in the night. Jaromir had been trained to focus on his other senses. He could hear the man's faint breath lurk nearer to him. He held his breath to listen to the noises. Sweat dripped down his neck, and a slight gust of winter tickled his ribs.

Click. A flame ignited in Jaromir's face, and the man's peering dark eyes and white face smirked in the orange glow. The fire danced and flickered with his malodorous breath. He held the flame with his thin palm and long fingers.

"I should kill you for what you've done!" Jaromir spat at him.

The pale-faced man smirked and sat on the table. His grin stretched up his aged face above the candlelight.

"I believe your position denies your ability to do so, Jaromir." He hovered the flame close to Jaromir's neck. "If it was the other way around, and if I was imprisoned. Would you let me free?"

Jaromir pondered on the question. An urge thrived in him to lie and save his own skin, but the words got stuck in his throat.

"I didn't think so," The hooded men retorted. He flicked his hood off, revealing his black mop hair and thin elongated face.

"You burnt my home and killed my parents!" Jaromir shouted. "You and Agustin…" The anger rushed through his body.

The flames haunted his dreams and crept around the corners of his mind. He had devoted his life to hunting down the person to avenge his parents, close the chapter of injustice and live a peaceful life. "You deserve to suffer like Agustin!" Jaromir could feel the sweat dripping down his neck with every movement of his head.

The large man set alight to the candles in the corner of the room. The row of candles rested on a downward angle and hung from the ceiling. Next to the man, Jaromir saw iron chains and a leather vest suspended from the ceiling and the wall.

The man clenched Jaromir's chin with his cold fingers and directed Jaromir's attention back to him, holding the flame in his other hand. "I had shared a lengthy amount of time with Agustin, but in the end, we both knew it was inevitable."

"Soon it'll be your turn, Pius."

"I think you're forgetting. You're the prisoner and I am the captor." The sorcerer edged the conjured flame closer to Jaromir's face. Jaromir stretched his neck away from it.

Pius snickered. "Have you asked your brother what happened to Tarnsby?"

Jaromir felt his heart thump. "I know it was you that burnt it down!" He took deep breaths and ramming his arms towards the sorcerer. "What have you done with Talmage? Where is he?"

"Don't act as if you care for your brother. You despise and disown him like a stray animal." He stood up and closed his hand. The flame puffed out as if there had been nothing.

It was true. Jaromir hadn't cared much about his twin brother. Zylah made sure of that before he went looking for him. *If I didn't go look for him, would I be here?* Jaromir reflected on his impulsive action to repair their kinship.

Jaromir watched the sorcerer stroll over to the row of lit candles. In the corner, the man rattled with chains and holding something significant that looked like a vest.

"Make sure it's ready," Pius mumbled to his servant before removing a candle from the shelf and walking back to Jaromir.

Under the small candle flame, hot liquid wax formed like a shallow pond.

Pius observed it. "This isn't your typical candle, Jaromir." He began, stepping in front of Jaromir and blocking his vision. "Chandlers and alchemists have been developing this unique form of candle for torture and the exclusive. Now for the first time in history, it will be used to change the world."

He slowly angled it over him. "Sometimes a little pain can spark the flame and conjure the memory like a dog cornered with nowhere to run, forced to search for its hereditary instinct and then, attack."

Drops of scorching hot wax sizzled onto Jaromir's torso. He restrained the urge to react to the burning pain, keeping his composure and staring at the man's black peering eyes. Pius frowned and pulled the candle upright, crouching down to observe the solidified wax within Jaromir's chest hairs. He smirked at him and gripped it with his long thin fingers. Pius yanked it out of Jaromir's chest. Ripping the hairs and skin off his chest. Jaromir held his composure. Pius frown and poured the rest of the melted wax on his neck and chin.

Jaromir couldn't withhold the pain any longer. Convulsing his chest and hips, jerking his constrained arms and legs—shifting from side to side, but the sorcerer held the candle flame close to his neck and continued to pour drops of hot wax onto his skin. Jaromir howled in pain. Pius' wicked laugh swirled in the darkroom.

Jaromir's breath slowed down after a short while, and the candle wax solidified around his neck. "How will this change the world? This will do nothing!"

"I know you sent messengers to seek an alliance. Where did you send them?"

Jaromir swallowed. His neck felt as if a hot knife sliced across it, encased with armor. He glared at the wrinkled malicious face.

"I know your games and plans, Jaromir. Make this easy for yourself and fill me in on what I don't know." Placing the candle on the wooden table, Pius leaned down, conjured the flame, and clenched his jaw.

Jaromir shrieked as his skin sizzled. The stench of burnt skin and hair stung his nostrils and tightened his throat. He struggled for air as he coughed and choked on the repulsive smell. The sorcerer grasped tighter.

Jaromir screamed from the pain, and his throat swelled like a frog, trying to break free.

Pius released his hand. Jaromir breathed deeply and shivered in agony.

His raw face tingled with each wheezing breath. "I'm not telling you anything, you filthy sorcerer," he whispered under his breath. "You'll never get away with this."

Pius pulled out the dagger from his waist. "If you keep running that tongue, I might have to remove it." He tested the sharpness with his thumb across the blade. It sliced it with ease, dripping blood down his thumb. "If I did that, how would I extract your secrets?" He sucked on the blood and pulled out a necklace from under his chest-plate and pressed his thumb onto it. He muttered something under his breath, and the wound closed over as if nothing had been there.

Pius leaned towards him. "The times are reverting to how they once were, my sweet primitive man. Before all the antimagicks rose to rule over the pure-blooded, Valenor and the Three Kingdoms were ruled by a Sorcerer Monarch, and it will soon relish again, but first, tell me where your men are heading!"

"I don't know where they are." He refused. It only will be a matter of time before Shaydin and Kadir were discovered. *I need more time.* "Valenor will never revert to magick." Each word floated from Jaromir's cracked lips, returning to Pius' plans.

"It's a funny story that I'll be very short with. You see, I trained to be a grand swordsman like you, and I wanted to rise through the ranks and gain my knighthood. But I couldn't. My body wasn't made for that. My long thin limbs and dangly body could never defeat my peers. It wasn't until then, I met Agustin. He didn't want to train anymore, and like me, he wanted to know about magick. Since then, we were bullied, beaten, and nearly killed by your kind, all for liking something other than weapons. Magick was our savior. It healed us, the wounded, and we soon discovered it wounds the condemned. It's the only way life should be. The world will revert to magick, whether you want it to or not, Jaromir."

Jaromir hadn't known about Agustin's past. *That's how he knew how to train me.* He reflected. Jaromir almost pitied them, but the fire that destroyed his parents burned in his memory. "What way of life is that?"

"A life of justice." Pius stood and straightened his robe. "Our past should not control our future. We must learn and grow from it. Wouldn't you agree?"

"Do you expect the people to bow to your commands?" Jaromir snapped. All his life, he had been chasing justice to claim his redemption.

"I devoted my life to mastering the art, but I never had the opportunity to sit upon the throne. People may not know this rugged face, but they know your face."

Jaromir shook his head, dumbfounded. "I'll never allow it."

"Your twin will. I've been grooming Talmage for years in secret to your pathetic order. He will serve as the new Sorcerer Monarch and deliver punishment to the unjustly—if he learns to bury his past."

"Agustin was the sorcerer, not Talmage!" He spat at him, refusing to believe the wicked sorcerer.

"Your order is Brother-in-Arms, yet Talmage hasn't been involved in any of its customs."

"So what? That doesn't mean he's able to rule Valenor and The Three Kingdoms."

"Your brother has felt the warmth of magic, and it's flowing through his veins. After he survives his trials, and with my aid, he shall have the opportunity to prove himself to the world and deliver justice to the unworthy." His hollow laugh filled the darkroom.

"Talmage would never practice the art of magick!" Jaromir refused to believe it, shouting over him.

Pius's nostrils flared as he peered at Jaromir. "You should've listened to your brother when you had the chance." His wicked laugh reverberated off the stone walls.

TALMAGE

A wheezing cough twisted his intestines. Talmage curled on the cold ground in the fetal position and spewed beside him. His throat burned, pressure squeezed on his head, and chunks of his last meal were stuck in his nasal cavity. He blew his nose and tried to sit up. His lungs were tender, and his arms throbbed. He forced his body upright. Managing to pull himself up, he rested his back upon the walls hard surface. Taking deep breaths and suppressing another round of spew, Talmage opened his eyes and scanned the darkness around him. He rubbed his stubble beard and stroked over his long wispy hair.

Talmage glanced at the darkness surrounding him. He cleared his throat and rubbed his head, trying to remember what happened before waking up. *Pius' face.* A soft icy breeze drifted around him. He forced himself to stand up and peer into the darkness. He cuffed his hands around his mouth to mimic a horn.

"Hello," Talmage called out. "Is anyone there?" His voice faded down into the nothingness.

He glanced upward to look for a climbing hole, but the passage walls were slightly higher than his head and as wide as his arms spread. He squinted and saw the passageway split in two directions.

Rummaging through his memories, the middle-aged man

rubbed the sides of his head. The damp air carried the fresh scent of winter and cold soil. The taste of bile and ale lingered in his mouth. He spat on the ground. Faint memories of his brother teaching him how to fight with a sword came to his mind. *Of all things, why am I remembering that?* Shifting his back on the jagged wall, he glanced in both directions.

His short sleeve tunic and breeches provided little warmth in the cold air. He shivered, and his exposed arm hairs stiffened. Rubbing them to keep warm, he shoved his hands in his pockets. Talmage searched through his pockets, patting his chest for the necklace with a streak of dread running through his mind. He shouted in anger. The artifact that was handed to him by Agustin was gone. His stomach eased, and his headache dissipated.

He tried to conjure a spell, swiveling his wrists to spark the flame, but a heavyweight pressed down on it as if an iron glove was on it. *There must be a magick ward here. Pius must've made these.*

Talmage put his hands on the cold stone sides of the tunnel and walked into the unknown. The echoing sounds of his boots slapped and his cough reverberated off the walls. He peered into the pitch-black before him. Talmage bellowed for help.

Talmage drifted through the darkness alone, rubbing his fingertips along the rock walls. He navigated and walked through the underground tunnel. His gaze slowly adjusted to the absence of light like a rodent.

Talmage glanced over his shoulder. He looked around him to see if any rocks he could use to carve a line in the wall. A loose pointy sharp rock lay close to the edge. Talmage picked it up and felt its edges. Testing it on the wall, Talmage engraved a "T" before continuing further into the passage. *If I can't use magick, this will do.*

He came to two diverging tunnels. Talmage stopped and pondered on his options and questioned the fact of him being stuck in the tunnels. He pounded the rock wall with his fist. The ceiling crumbled; small rocks bounced on his shoulders. *Is this Pius' last piece of his plan? To get rid of me. He should've just killed me, then, I could be with everyone.*

When he was young, he lost his parents. The fire he somehow conjured, perished every person he loved and cared about, except Jaromir. He didn't dare tell his brother how it started, and the aching remorse hung on his shoulders.

Jaromir had taken care of him as they left the scorched village and ventured towards the capitol, Valenor. Not long after they had left Tarnsby, they had encountered a merchant, Agustin, and he had safeguarded Talmage and Jaromir on their journey.

If I had said something back then, things would've been different.

Talmage stood. His vision had adjusted, but he could see no farther than three feet ahead in either direction.

A cold wind floated from one of the openings, carrying the soft sounds of a girl crying.

"Who's there?" His dry croaky voice trailed down the emptiness. Talmage rubbed his dry eyes and licked his parched lips. The sobbing grew louder. "Stay there! I'm coming." He stumbled down the passage to where he assumed the voice came. He called out, but nothing. Walking blindly in the dark passage, rubbing his hand along the wall and a hand in front, Talmage began trekking.

"Why the change of heart, Talmage?" A womanly voice floated from up ahead.

He stopped. Talmage recognized the voice. *It can't be.* His hands trembled, and his breaths were shallow and fast.

"You never did help me. You lied to me and played as a fool!"

Talmage refused to believe it. She began crying, but it faded away from him. Talmage ran after the sound. "Bethany! I'm coming for you."

"Don't follow me!" She screamed at him. "You never wanted to talk to me. All you did was…" Her voice trailed off.

Talmage ran after her, dropping the rock and chasing her voice. Down passages, through the openings, and following the soft sobbing. *She can't be here.* "Bethany! Stop running! I need you…" Talmage's breath wheezed as he stumbled after her. His chest was tightening with each breath. A faint hazy glow caught his eye up ahead. He ran towards it, with his arms out, pressing the walls. He stumbled around a bend.

"You never needed me." Bethany stood before him, just as she looked when he had seen her last.

Talmage could feel his heart beating in his chest. Bethany hovered with an illuminating white glow, like an angel. Her short messy brown hair fell onto one of her shoulders. She looked no different to the day when Talmage found her, hanging from a rope. The rope wasn't around her snapped neck but the marks wrapped around her skin. Her white dress was stained with dirt and blood.

"How… how are you here?" Talmage stuttered.

"It's not important how I got here."

"Of course, it's important! You're dead." Talmage's pulse throbbed in his throat, and his palms sweated. "I cradled you when I untied you. I felt your last breath…"

"This is your fault!" She screamed, her head still sloping to her shoulder. Her stained yellow teeth glared at him with each word. "You made me do this."

He shook his head. "You're not real. You can't be here."

"Is this real enough for you?" She glided towards him, gusting an earthy aroma over him. Her feet hung slightly off above the ground, and she gripped his neck with her cold hand. Icy coldness ran through Talmage's body. He slipped out of her grip and stepped away from her.

"Why are you here?" He asked softly to her. He couldn't look into her large pupils. Scared of his past, the day he had seen her hanging in her home haunted his dreams. Some nights he questioned whether it was his fault, and if he arrived home earlier, he could have saved her.

"I'm here to remind you that your past will always be with you." She pointed her finger at his heart. "Just as my awful life always haunted me. I loved you, Talmage."

Talmage's throat tightened. "I'm sorry, Bethany. I still love you. I dream of you every night."

"I can't love someone that lied and abandoned my trust," she said.

Her words stabbed his heart. She knew about his secret. As Talmage went to apologize, she pressed her cold finger on his lips. "Don't bother. Live with your past, and don't let it control your future. A supreme ruler has no ghosts haunting him. You must be as cold as my touch."

Talmage frowned. Bethany straightened her neck and lowered to the ground. She turned and strolled further into the passageway. Talmage watched her hair change shape, her legs covered by clothes, and her size grow. Bethany faced him, but it wasn't her anymore. She took the form of a man. A man that Talmage recognized. He stood in a black robe, and his dark hair slicked back behind his ears. "Survive this, Talmage, and you shall rule The Three Kingdoms."

Darkness swept past him, and the light disappeared. Talmage stood in the antimagick passages, alone. He took a deep breath with one hand leaned on the wall. Sweat dripped off his face, and he   spat   the   lingering   bile   on   the   ground.

JAROMIR

"Talmage would never practice magick. Where is he? What have you done with him?" Jaromir demanded.

"Don't act as if you care. The damage is done," Pius said, short and blunt. "Tell me where you sent your messengers."

Pius leaned over Jaromir holding the candle, reflecting his pale face against the orange glow. *He's right. I wasted all that time with Talmage when he needed me the most. Should I tell him our plans?* Jaromir contemplated, staring at the sorcerer.

Pius turned and nodded at his servant before Jaromir could answer. The large man stood at the end of the table with the chains wrapped around his hands.

He tightened the chain, yanked Jaromir's ankles and wrists, and spreading them further away from his body. His shoulders and knees cracked and popped. Jaromir shrieked in agony, crying, and thrusting his hips as the cuffs dug into his skin. His torso muscles pulled away from the center of his body.

He screamed, before clenching his teeth and trying to disperse the pain surging through his body. "What do you want to know?"

"You know what I want. Tell me where you sent the alliance."

The pain Jaromir endured ran through his body, but he knew, if the world was full of magick, he'd suffer even more. "Tell me where Talmage is."

Pius laughed. "You want to play that game with me. Fine. Morten, bring her in." He gestured to his servant standing in the shadows. Heavy thuds moved further away, and it swung the door open. Jaromir peered at the faint gray light. His heart throbbed under the molded wax.

A womanly scream grew louder.

Morten appeared in the doorway, carrying someone with long hair. She jerked and tossed around, punching the man, but Morten's strength was beyond her defense.

"Let go of me!" The woman shouted and kicked him. She struggled with Morten carrying her into the darkroom, against her will. Her long hair swayed as she tossed and squirmed on his shoulders to release herself from the large man's grip. Jaromir peered through the shadow of the light, and immediately, the woman caught his vision.

Jaromir's heart dropped. "Zylah! What are you doing to her? Let go of her!" Jaromir cried out as the servant dragged her in the room and over to the corner.

She thrashed about, kicking, and screaming as Morten forced the leather vest over her arms.

Pius laughed while he slammed the door shut. He ambled towards Morten, as the servant tightened the buckles around Zylah's chest and locking the shackles around her ankles and wrists. The candle flames flickered, revealing the anger in her face.

"Leave her out of it!" Jaromir bellowed. "Why have you brought her here?"

"You see, Jaromir, as much as I want to leave her out of it. I couldn't. I simply couldn't leave her out of this dilemma, just as much as she couldn't stay out of it. Do you see my conflict?"

Jaromir watched the wicked sorcerer. His disheveled hair glistened, and his narrow black eyes beamed at him.

"Do you want to know why she's here?" Pius pressed the issue without giving him a chance to answer. "She told me that you know all of my secrets."

"You don't have to drag her into this. It's me you want. Not her!"

"How much do you know about Zylah?"

Jaromir shook his head. "I know her more than you do!"

"Interesting," Pius sneered. "How do you think I knew you

were heading to the Amalgamate, last night?"

Jaromir glanced at his wife as she flailed in the leather vest. Betrayal ran through his body. *How could she? Of all the things I've done to protect her.*

Pius hovered closer to him and continued. "For a long time, you've been killing my people and searching for me, but I guess I won our little cat and mouse game." Pius gestured to Morten with his long arms.

Morten paced from Zylah's side and to the end of the table. He pulled down on the lever and tightened the chains around the circular mechanism.

A slight glow came from the corner where his wife was imprisoned. Jaromir glanced over, but Morten stiffened the slack of his chains.

Jaromir's shoulders popped.

He shrieked in pain.

His cries reverberated in the darkroom. Taking deep breaths in between each bellowing howl, he tried to pull his arms closer to the center of his body to stop them from snapping off, but they didn't respond.

"That's enough," Pius ordered.

Jaromir's body flopped onto the wooden plank. The tension ceased, but his arms were limp. He wriggled his fingers and toes to confirm they were still attached.

Jaromir searched the small room for his wife. The well sat in the opposite corner, and the candles flickered, casting shadows up the wall. Underneath the chains extending from the ceiling, Zylah hung forward, and wax dripped onto her head. It molded around her scalp and weaved through her hair, forging long thin tapering pieces of wax down either side of her head. Suspended behind her were multiple candles hanging from the ceiling on an angle and dripping wax directly onto her head. Zylah screamed and thrashed her head back and forth. The wax carried small flames onto her scalp and shoulders.

The horrific scene stole the little breath Jaromir had left. A wave of burning anger circulated through his aching limbs. Jaromir thrust his body forward, trying to break free from the chains, but he failed.

"Stop it!" He cried out.

Pius crouched down at eye level to Jaromir. "Don't you like

seeing your wife covered in the wax? Her sculpture could turn out to be a piece of beautiful art, much better than what I could make with my magick." His hollow laugh filled the darkness.

"You filthy piece of shit." Jaromir's words morphed into shrieks of anguish as Morten pulled on the mechanism, tearing his arms away towards the walls.

The sorcerer's laugh was smothered by the prisoner's desperate cries for liberation. Consumed by agony and suffering, Jaromir slumped onto the table as Morten released the chains' tension.

Jaromir flopped his head to the side.

"You know what I want and so does she." Pius stood above him, holding the candle. His smile stretched across his hairless face.

Jaromir scrunched his face. "I don't know your plans," he replied with a soft, weak voice.

"Surely you remember telling her, don't you?" Pius walked over to Zylah.

Zylah had collapsed to her knees in the corner; the leather vest with belt buckles strapped across her chest and held her arms above her head. Wax covered her head and shoulders. It dripped down the back of her hair, hardening her neck like frozen icicles. She lifted her head. It cracked and crumbled with her movements as more wax leaked onto her, covering the newly made crevices. Deep dark circles hung from her eyes, and tears streamed down her face like The Cleave River that parted the three kingdoms.

Jaromir's throat tightened, and his heart beat faster. "Why did you bring her into this?"

"Is it hard to see your loved one in an immense amount of pain?" Pius hunched over. He studied Zylah's face and the wax over her body. "Morten ease up on the candles. At this rate, she'll be a sculpture before the night's over."

Morten walked with heavy steps, thudding the ground, over to the candles, and removed two of the six hanging above Zylah. His thick arms and wide legs stood under his broad body, and the shadow of the flames danced on his grotesque face. His beady black eyes studied the light with caution as he moved it to the torch fixtures on the wall.

"See, my dear friend," Pius stood and shuffled towards the table, his robe drifting behind him like an ominous stormy cloud. "I know you don't care about her. She told your brother numerous times. Oh yes, they've been communicating for quite a while now, haven't you known that? This is a little awkward, isn't it, Zylah?"

Jaromir jerked to grab the sorcerer, but the chains stopped him. He clenched his jaw in fury and took a deep breath. "Stop spinning your web of lies! Don't act like you know her!"

"Denial could be your downfall, Jaromir. If you only accepted the truth of the world around you, you would be a much happier man," Pius answered with a gentle tone.

"I know my truth!" Jaromir forced himself towards the sorcerer standing over him, grinning.

"Do you?" Pius leaned closer to him.

The words pierced Jaromir like an ice shard penetrating his chest. He glanced at Zylah. "Is it true?" Jaromir directed his question to his wife.

She took deep husky breaths. "What else was I meant to do? You never paid any attention to me!"

"Why didn't you tell me you were speaking to Talmage?"

"You wouldn't have listened to me! You were so consumed in planning your raids and your fucking order!" Zylah coughed, and her chains rattled.

"I was doing it to protect everyone. To protect you! I wanted to make the world a safer place!" Jaromir's veins throbbed in his neck from shouting at her.

"Both of you shut it," Pius interjected. "You're both giving me a headache." He rubbed his temples before he continued. "You see, as I was mentioning before, you and Zylah are in a peculiar situation. You sent messengers for an alliance to overthrow me, but my men only stopped one of your men. Where is your other messenger?"

Jaromir gazed in silence.

Pius leaned closer. "Words can spread like a virus—infectious and contagious to vulnerable people. Some people idle past, and the virus is unable to attach. Soon enough, the more people that are exposed to the virus—the higher the chance of an infection rate. Most of the time after the virus disseminates, the source of it is hard to discover, but in this case, when a co-existing virus has spread, it leads a trail directly back to you." Pius straightened his back and inflated his chest with an extensive breath. He vented his frustrations, calming himself before continuing.

"I don't call myself a qualified physician. I never have, Jaromir, believe me, but when an infectious virus is starting to spread, it prevents an apprentice Sorcerer Monarch from coming to rule and forces an army of primitive men waltzing through the streets. I need to find the infection at the beginning before it mutates and spreads to vulnerable people. In time, I will be the best-unqualified physician in The Three Kingdoms."

Jaromir was too frightened to speak. His captor was unpredictable, and his face was expressionless. An overload of information baffled Jaromir.

"What do you want me to tell you?" He finally pleaded. Jaromir had searched his memories.

"Tell him, Jar. Please, I'm sorry for sneaking behind your back, but I don't want to die!" Zylah begged from under the molten wax. Her weak voice pleaded for mercy.

Pius spun around and kneeled next to Zylah. "Who gave you the impression you'll make it out of here alive? Even if your husband discloses where he sent his men and we remove the infectious words from the kingdoms, there's a strong chance you won't make it out alive." He laughed at the prisoner's predicament. His twisted and malicious proposal did not entice Jaromir but infuriated him.

"You need to tell me!" Pius shouted, breaking Jaromir's thoughts. "You and your damned order can burn in hell!" Pius paced over to Jaromir and stood face-to-face with him. His breath reeked of sulfur and rotten carcass.

Jaromir scowled at him. Pius flattened the crease in his robe. "I have one of your messengers, but you don't have much time to save him and everyone else."

"Where's Talmage?" Jaromir demanded.

"Somewhere stuck in the layers of his subconscious." Pius sniggered. "His magick is useless down there unless I intervene. He has to resort to primitive thinking, but if he proves himself, he'll be worthy of sitting on the throne."

"Talmage would never go against his family!" Jaromir bellowed.

"Do you think Agustin wouldn't have taught Talmage? The sooner you accept the truth, the sooner you will die in peace."

The thought of Pius telling him Talmage had been practicing magick infuriated him. Magick had destroyed their village and killed their parents. Talmage never spoke about it. At times, Jaromir tried to talk about it but Talmage refused to express his true feelings.

Pius grinned at him before opening the stone door. Another

troll-man stood in the doorframe. "It's about time you came, Renold." He said in an annoyed tone. "Do you put him down there?"

Renold grunted and moaned.

"Never mind. Get to work." Pius let him enter and nodded at Morten.

Both servants gripped a lever at each end of the table and pulled down on it, turning the gears. It yanked the chains and whipped Jaromir's ankles and his wrists. His joints popped, and his shoulders stretched above his head. Jaromir screamed into the cold dark room.

TALMAGE

Alone.

Heartbroken.

Talmage had suffered enough. He tried to forget all his sorrows at the Amalgamate and now to see his dead lover again. His heart ached. *Was that real?* He had felt her cold touch and smelt her lavender aroma.

Talmage shook as he hunched over, breathing deeply. Grief had stricken him with Bethany's presence but raged boiled in him for being deceived by his mentor. *Why would he torment me?*

"Why?" Talmage shouted. He thought he had moved on and accepted the fact that he would never say goodbye or sorry, but it seemed his ghosts were still haunting him. He had tried to live without her. Talmage told Pius after it happened, he was the only person Talmage could rely on.

Talmage slammed his fist into the rock wall. *Live with your past.* "I live with it every fucking day." He muttered. He hadn't taken note of where he ran while chasing after his dead lover and now, he seemed even more lost than before. *What else does that prick have waiting for me?*

He swallowed his anger and focused on his predicament. He had to escape from Pius' last trial. As he caressed his stubble beard, he noticed the walls. They were different than before. They had changed from bare rocks, now, to hairy moss and smothering vines along the walls.

Talmage began walking, rubbing his hand along the rough edges of the thick tree root. The labyrinth of diverging tunnels stretched further away in the darkness. Talmage tried to ignite a flame in his hand, but the ward weaved its power around him. His hands trembled at the thought of the tunnels becoming his tomb. The cool breeze he had once felt faded, and now a damp soil scent smothered his body and wafted into his lungs.

Talmage stopped and inspected the ceiling. The glistening rocks shimmered as if the rock seeped blood from its wounds. His stomach growled, and the taste of bile lingered in his mouth.

I wonder if Jaromir is looking for me. His brother never took the time to take an interest in his life or noticed he was alive anymore. When he was younger, Pius had informed him that his brother had started arcane work for the Empress. To try to eradicate all magick users from the kingdoms. Talmage disowned his brother and leaned more towards the magick Agustin had taught him. Jaromir despised magick and thought it was the root of all evil, but that caused Talmage to worship it even more.

He had kept his magick lessons secret from Jaromir because he knew his brother wanted revenge on all the sorcerers for the blame of burning down their village. *If only he knew the truth.*

Pius showed Talmage the true meaning of justice, social order, and the art of magick. As they grew older, Jaromir moved to the confined walls of Valenor, and Talmage remained on the other side, close to the Amalgamate. Jealousy and hatred brewed in Talmage for his twin brother, as Jaromir rose in knighthood ranks and defended the city from invading armies and sorcerers.

Talmage never learned the art of swordsmanship, but Jaromir had perfected it. The lust for revenge and hatred for magick users fueled his twin brother and encouraged him to be invincible with any dagger, short, or long sword. Often, Talmage had watched Jaromir train in the fields and visualized them going head-to-head, sword against fire; primitive against magickal.

Talmage smiled at the thought before he yelled out. "Hello? Is anyone in here?" No voices answered, but except the echo of his voice, fading into the endless blackness.

He continued through the underground passage.

For a while, Talmage paced deeper into the passage, dwelling on possible ghosts. *Could he really choose him?* Talmage suppressed the thought.

Talmage's wheezing cough, and his dry mouth cracked his lips. He tried to moisten them, but they were parched. Drops of water dripped from the overhanging vines. He stretched his hands and scraped off some of the moss and sniffed it. He cringed at the damp scent, but he knew it would keep him alive.

Talmage shoved it in his mouth and chewed. Rocks crunched on his teeth, and the furry leaves grazed his gums. Imagining roast chicken with its small bones and skin to make it more tolerable. Grabbing more of the moss, he shoved handfuls into his pocket. Underneath the moss on the ceiling, trickles of water hung off the rocks. He rubbed his calloused fingertips along it and tasted it. There was a slight metal and soil flavor.

Again, he swiped his hands across the roof, getting minuscule amounts of liquid, slowly easing his parched mouth, scoop by scoop. Talmage ripped part of his linen shirt off and used the vines to stand and climb higher. Reaching off the ground and pressing his shirt on the roof, he collected all the water his weakening legs allowed. He patted his face with his shirt, with small rocks jabbing into his face. Talmage didn't care. The moistened shirt on his skin eased his dehydrated face.

The reinvigorated man laughed. Laughing into his shirt, a wave of ridiculousness and exhaustion weighed on his shoulders. A burst of crazed laughter possessed him and morphed into an outbreaking howl into his shirt.

"Help! Is anyone there?" He bellowed, listening to his voice fade down into the darkness. "Help!"

No one appeared, and no one heard Talmage lost in the dark labyrinth of moist rocks.

JAROMIR

Morten and Renold lowered the poles. Tears poured from Jaromir's eyes as the cogs turned and stretched his limbs.

"Please! Stop!" He begged, pleading for his life.

His arms slowly extended from his shoulders, his back muscles spread towards the walls, and his torso strained with each pull of the chain.

Jaromir shrieked in agony, opening his eyes, and seeing the vile sorcerer leaning over and staring at him. In one hand, the sorcerer held a stone and a flame in the other.

"Please stop!" Jaromir pleaded.

Pius revealed a thin smile from his wiry bearded face and nodded at the two brutes at either end of the table. The chain dropped its slack, and Jaromir's arms and legs fell with a thud onto the wood. He tried to lift his arms, but his arms were weak and limp.

Zylah sobbed. Her erratic quiet breaths hung in the room, and her chains jingled in the darkness. Pius hovered over Jaromir like a shadow.

Underneath the pain and sorrow, Jaromir's heart sunk. "Leave her out of it. She hasn't done anything."

"Well, this is where the narrative twists and the plot thickens.

You see, while you were unconscious, Zylah did tell me something quite different to what you've told me." Pius's voice whispered over the soft flame. The fire stood firm from his villainous breath and flickered as if it was groveling like a submissive animal. "Didn't you?" He held the flame over Zylah.

Unconscious? I must've blacked out. Jaromir was dumbfounded. His memory did seem fuzzy and his eyes felt swollen as he looked at Zylah.

Shadows hung on her face as she tilted her head upwards. Solid yellow wax molded over her scalp, drooping in front of her face like icicles in a cavern. Her dark, saddened eyes stared at Jaromir from behind the wax.

What did she tell him?

Pius turned around and gestured to one of his servants to come to his aid. Jaromir lifted his wrists, but his elbows remained stuck to the table. His muscles lacked their strength to fight against his captor. Morten stomped towards Pius. The servant grabbed Zylah and ripped her head back to face the ceiling, the wax snapping off her head. She screamed and kicked her legs around, trying to break free.

The other servant paced over and clasped her flailing arms, while Morten whipped her neck backward to face the ceiling, again. Her mouth opened, and her chin sunk into her neck.

"What are you doing? What have you told them, Zylah?" Jaromir shrieked. He lifted his chest to escape from the restraints. With a renewed strength, he surged towards them, trying to break free and save his wife from the foreboding matter.

Pius unbuckled the leather vest, revealing the top of her chest. Zylah squirmed, but the two servants tightened their grips.

"Leave her alone!" Jaromir cried out.

The sorcerer winked at him. Jaromir broke into a fury, jolting his bruised and flabby arms, trying to break the chains off. Pius grabbed one of the suspended candles and tilted it over her. It dripped scorching wax over her chest. She screamed and thrashed about, and the two brutes constrained her. For what felt like an eternity, Jaromir attempted to escape, but the wicked sorcerer and his servants tortured his wife.

"If I ever get out of this, you'll be sorry! All of you! Especially you, Pius!" Jaromir couldn't hold back his frustration and anger. For years he had trained and sought revenge on Pius for burning his home. The vile, wicked man stood before him torturing his wife, and he could do nothing about it.

The two men dropped Zylah. She hung from the vest, suspended from the ground, her arms stretched towards the ceiling as her head dangled. Pius turned his head to Jaromir. His piercing black eyes glared at him. The sorcerer straightened his back and gestured to his servants to move away from the sobbing and suffering woman. Jaromir took deep breaths. Anticipating the sorcerer's next dangerous action. He watched Pius sit on the table. "Let us leave, please?" Jaromir's words trailed off. His rage subsided, Jaromir mulled on speaking with reason and if the sorcerer would let him free and fill the void of revenge.

"You just told us that we'd be sorry if you get out of here. I know you conspired with the Empress to rid us from humanity, and you want your revenge." Pius grinned at him. "Why would I let you leave?"

Jaromir clenched his jaw. "I'll withdraw my men, and we'll act as if nothing happened here."

"As intriguing as your offer is, a hint of deceit and betrayal hangs in your voice."

"You have my word."

"What word is that? The words of an antimagick orphan raised by a sorcerer? Don't mock me, boy. Agustin was a dear friend of mine, and you killed him and tried to blame it on us. Although," he said with a lighter tone. "He did introduce me to your brother. Talmage does show some potential, and he excelled at a faster rate than most, but his self-sabotage will be his downfall. Nevertheless, he could lead the kingdoms to greatness with my help."

Jaromir had killed Agustin in his own home. Jaromir discovered Agustin was a sorcerer. His order infiltrated one of their hideouts and found out that Agustin was a sorcerer. Jaromir commanded his men to retreat, and he hunted his guardian. At first, he was heartbroken, but he stayed true to his belief and blamed him for the murder of his parents. The next day, Jaromir snuck into Agustin's home. Agustin stood in the center of his house, waiting for Jaromir.

Agustin fell to his knees, with his hands around his back, exposing his throat to finish the job. Inner turmoil fought in Jaromir, but he had been obedient to the order and The Three Kingdoms. Before he took Agustin's life, his last words lingered. "I knew you were going to kill me one day. It's the reason I trained you in weaponry."

"Stop it. Stop spinning your lies about Talmage!" Jaromir yelled at Pius, breaking from his past. "I know what you're doing, and it's not working!"

"I would never speak lies, but you, on the other hand… I highly doubt you were speaking the truth when you told Talmage how Agustin died." Pius glared at him, his face covered in deep pores and pale scars. His wide sharp nose bulged from his face in the dim light. Sweat formed in Jaromir's palms, and he swallowed the built-up saliva.

"You have my word, and if you free us, I'll pull back all my men. I promise." Jaromir squirmed and arched his back in frustration. "I won't tell anyone about what happened here. No one will come after you." As he spoke, he could feel the desperation in his voice.

Pius chuckled. "I want the world to know what happened here today. I want everyone to know, the leader of the rebellion begged for his life."

"You're deranged! Let us out of here!" Jaromir thrashed around as Pius' malicious cackle filled the cold dark room. "I'll do anything," he mumbled under his breath.

The sorcerer fell silent. "Anything?" Pius's voice was lighter and calmer.

Jaromir opened his eyes. As he studied Pius's wicked grin, he wished he hadn't said it, but it was too late. Jaromir nodded.

"There is a certain thing a person in your position could accomplish for me."

"If I do it, do I have your word that you'll set us all free?"

"When have I lied to you?" Pius answered.

Everything you said about Talmage. Jaromir wanted to answer but knew this was his one chance to escape, and knowing that Pius was setting him free, he withheld the truth and stayed silent.

"Hmm. Very well." Pius turned and gestured to his servants to set him free.

Morten and Renold began unlocking the shackles around his ankles and wrists. The heavyweights that sunk into Jaromir's body slowly lifted with each jingle of the chain.

As the servants placed their hands on the chains, a surge of vigor filtered through his body. *I only have one chance.* Jaromir decided, watching them lift his arms to unravel the chains. *I need to inform Empress Suiko.*

Pius held up his hand. "Stop." The two brutes waited for their master. "What kind of fool do you take me? How could I trust you? You must think I'm an idiot! Double lock the chains this time. Let's hope it teaches him humility."

"Please don't!" Jaromir begged and thrashed his arms to break free, but the men forced him down. Zylah screamed and cried in the shadows.

"Tell me who your messengers were! Who are your alliances? It'll save all this nonsense! The Three Kingdoms could be mine, but instead, I'm dealing with this ridiculousness..." Pius cleared his throat and caressed his forehead. He saw the candle flames above Zylah and sat next to Jaromir as the two men locked his wrists and ankles. The cold pressure of the iron strangled his limbs. *The kingdoms will be his? Doesn't he want Talmage to rule?* Jaromir pondered on his words. *I need to save Tal. He'll be Pius' puppet.* Jaromir thought. He studied the sorcerer's eyes; they were like two dark pools of water that glimmered from the flame in his hand. Magick had never interested Jaromir, but as his gaze fell upon the flame, a warm feeling filled his body, a sense of hope. *Is this the touch of magick?* Thoughts of his brother delving into the art rose in his mind. The questions and guilt weighed on him.

Pius paced to the wall and grabbed the tongs from it and examined them in the light. He suddenly seized Jaromir's jaw.

Jaromir tossed his head, trying to beat him off, but the sorcerer brushed it off like a bug pestering him. "I know how to keep you alive so you can suffer from the most glorious pain imaginable." Pius opened Jaromir's bottom jaw. Jaromir tossed his head back and forth, releasing his grip. "You're like a fucking worm. Stay still!" Pius forced Jaromir down. Her cry for mercy echoed behind them.

"Never!" Jaromir thrashed about, doing everything possible to stay free from more torture.

Pius raced to the wall and grabbed a clamp and a leather belt. "This'll stop you moving." He wrapped the belt over Jaromir's body and tightened it. Unwinding the clamp, he placed it over Jaromir's head.

Jaromir tried to break free from his grip, lifting his head, trying to move his head away from the enclosing brackets to his temple.

"What do you want?" He shouted.

Pius continued turning the handle, tightening the clamps jaw with a smile on his face.

"I'll tell you where I sent my men!" Jaromir admitted.

Pius stopped. Standing over him with his hand clasped onto the handle and frame. It was just touching his temples. "Go on," Pius said in a calm and gentle voice.

Jaromir panted. "I sent word to Ashwood with my comrades, Hunter and Edgar," he lied. Hunter and Edgar were two of the youngest brothers-in-arms for the cause against the sorcerers.

"Now was it that hard to tell me that? You could've avoided all this suffering if you told me sooner." Pius smiled and nodded.

He bought it. Jaromir tried to move his head. The clamps squeezed tight on his head as a grape stomped for its juices.

Pius leaned closer to Jaromir's face. "No, it wasn't that hard to lie to me, was it? You need to realize your truth. Hunter and Edgar have been killed, just like your parents. I am not a fool, but it seems you think I am!" Pius squeezed the clamp on his head.

Squeezing his head together but not too tight and grabbing tongs. Thoughts of the two young men burning in flames, screaming for their life.

"I'm sorry. I'm sorry!" Jaromir tried to rip his head free, trying to thrash his head out of the clamp. Pius stood over him with a thin grin stretching across his face. He let go of Jaromir's tongue.

His tongue was swollen from the hot iron. He did not have the strength to answer.

Pius chuckled and turned around. "Everyone's fate is in your control. Don't throw their lives away because of your pride. Suiko was leading our people to chaos and ruin—I serve the kingdoms and my art. You must respect that." Pius nodded and gestured for Morten and Renold to grab each pole at the table's head and feet.

Jaromir was tired. He had suffered a vast amount of pain. He hung on with his life, and at times almost, he wanted to admit defeat. His comrades weren't there to save him like they had before. Now, if he died, he didn't care. He would rather be tortured to death than see his wife suffer the same fate if it was to save everyone.

"Do you think I won't do the same to them as I have done to you? Your ego will kill you all, and it will be your soul that falls into a limbo between the realms of gods and devils. You will forever be sleepless and exhausted."

"Why haven't you killed us already?" Jaromir mumbled, coughing up blood.

"What was that?" Pius gestured to the brutes to stop. He leaned closer, holding the tongs in his face.

It was a gamble Jaromir was willing to risk. If the sorcerer ended his suffering, he might save his wife. He repeated the question without coughing.

"It intrigues me that you ask. If it isn't obvious, I guess I must explain it to your simple mind. If I killed you, then I wouldn't know where you sent your messages. For now, I must take care of something else." Pius grabbed a candle and placed it close to Jaromir's torso. The heat from the flame gently touched his skin. "Until then, don't let the light go out." Pius stood and left the room. Morten and Renold followed their master, leaving him alone with his wife.

TALMAGE

Talmage rested. His eyes watered, and his wheezing cough closed his throat. He glanced at the tunnel stretching at the distance. A faint light reflected on the plants. He rubbed his neck and sighed.

Before him, open passages stretched out like roots, heading in a nonsensical and inconsistent pattern. The moss and vines seemed to follow down one opening. Talmage shifted in his damp shirt, the moisture seeped into his skin, and a cool breeze tingled his spine. Talmage's stomach rumbled as he scanned the darkness. He grabbed a handful of moss and forced it down his throat before following the vines.

"Hello? Is anyone there?" Talmage called out.

Nothing answered but the sound of his boots grazing over the roots and rocks. Crumbling stones faded into the blackness, and a thick damp smell filled the tight space. His vision had slowly adjusted to the dim surroundings. He carefully stepped over the uneven ground and walked around the bends, following the roots that weaved like slithering snakes.

Talmage reached a point in the passage where it opened to an underground cave with a small pond. Around the edges, the vines continued and ran through an opening up above at the cave's highest point. Talmage stood in awe. The murky water was like a clear sky during twilight with swirls of deep blues and purples, and a scent of freshness and soil-filled the air. All of a sudden, his wheezing cough flared, and he uncontrollably hacked into his hand. His lungs tensed, and his throat tightened as if someone were strangling him. He had always wondered why he was cursed with a wheezing cough instead of his twin brother. He slowed his breathing to calm his convulsions.

"Drink some of this. It'll help your throat." A man's voice said.

Talmage twisted his head around to see a figure crouching at the edge of the water. He peered at the man. "Who're you?"

"I thought you'd recognize me." The man approached him. He wore a long black robe and a weathered tunic. A thick open gash ran around his throat like a necklace.

Talmage rose. "It... It can't be."

"Have this water. It'll help your throat." The man offered.

"I know it's you, Pius. Stay away from me!" Talmage rummaged his hands on the ground, picking up a rock. He held it above his head, ready to throw it at him. "Leave me alone! Agustin's dead. Let him rest." Talmage threw the rock, but it went straight through him. He turned to run.

"There's no point, Tal. I'm here to help you. I know how you suffer every day."

"You know nothing about me, Pius!"

Agustin drifted towards him. He didn't have a glow like Bethany, but he wore the same thing the day he died like her. "It's me. Your guardian, Agustin."

Talmage lost his breath. Only Agustin had referred to himself as his guardian. His heart had yearned for him ever since his death. He can't remember much of his parents, but Agustin had been like a father to him. "Are you here to haunt me?"

Agustin laughed and drifted closer to him. "Don't be stupid and trust me. Drink from the lake. It's safe."

Talmage hesitantly crouched to the water, scooped it up, and sniffed it before slurping it out of his hand. It was salty, but the cold liquid soothed his throat. Talmage shoved his face in it and drank until he was bloated. He sat back and sighed.

"Feel better?"

Talmage nodded. "So, why are you here?"

"I could ask you the same question."

That's something he'd say. Talmage smirked. "At first, I knew why, but now I'm not sure."

"What was that?"

"I thought I wanted to be a ruler, but now, I don't know."

Agustin sat down beside him. Both absently observed at the murky underground lake. "Our minds are like this water, Tal. From a distance, it can seem like this grand mystical body of water. But all these small elements to create this lake have endured a lifetime of hardship. Little things are easily blind to the passing stranger. Breathe and focus, Talmage. Take the time to think about what you want for your body of water. Then, what you want can be apparent." Agustin swirled his hand above the water.

The murky lake cleared, and the reflection of Talmage stared back at him. He remembered how much he was an identical twin, apart from the different eye colors. The narrow face covered with a shirt stubble beard. *Maybe I shouldn't resent Jaromir. He's the only family left.*

Talmage lifted his gaze toward Agustin. He longed for a hug of him, any form of real affection. His heart throbbed in his throat as he listened to his guardian speak.

"I'll repeat my question, Talmage. Why are you here?"

For a while, Talmage thought on his answer. He was confused. Finally, he answered. "I need to undo the wrong I've done."

Agustin laughed. "You haven't done anything wrong. You did what was right at the time. Think of all the wrong Jaromir has done. All the people he killed, all the innocent lives he stole, all because he can't break away from his past. Your first act of magick might've murdered your parents, but who took my life?"

Talmage frowned. "Who took your life?"

"I think you know. You just saw him." Agustin began walking away, and Talmage jumped and reached for his shoulder to spin him around. He stumbled across the rocks. *Jaromir couldn't have killed him. He loved him as much as I did.* He watched Agustin's black flowing cape fade into the dark passageway, leaving him alone with the clear water.

JAROMIR

"Jar! Are you okay?" Zylah's voice shrieked from the darkness, carrying fear and anxiety. Her chains rattled as she tried to move closer to him.

Jaromir rose and saw that the wax over Zylah's scalp had begun to break off. He wriggled his torso and his wrists. His arms gained little strength, and his legs were weak. The candle flickered against his skin, casting a soft glowing heat.

"I'm here." Jaromir cleared his throat. "I'm fine. I shouldn't have left my plans so loosely around our home. This is my fault we're both in here." Jaromir's throat tightened, and his heart ached for how much pain she had suffered.

"I'm glad you're alive." She shook her head, breaking off more wax from around her face.

Jaromir squinted and tried to sit up, but his arms were weak. Zylah straightened her back and glanced around the room.

"How long have you been speaking with Talmage?" Jaromir interrogated.

Zylah cleared her throat. "I'm not sure."

"Tell me!" Jaromir commanded.

"For a few years." Zylah obeyed.

"A few years?"

"It was on and off. Jaromir, you neglected your brother. Your own flesh and blood. Have you once thought about how Talmage might be feeling?"

"Why didn't you tell me?"

"I tried to, but your head was stuck up your ass! You never listen to me!"

Jaromir could hear her deep breathing. "I'm sorry, Zylah. When we get out? Things will be different, I promise."

"I hope we get out of here." Her voice was cold as stone.

Me too. "What did you tell him?" Jaromir demanded.

"I told him everything I knew."

Jaromir sighed. *There are things you don't know.* "What exactly did you tell him?"

"I told him you sent messengers for an alliance with the other kingdoms."

"What messengers did you tell him?" Jaromir was growing irritated.

"Only Kadir."

A sudden coldness hit Jaromir in the core of his body. His skin tingled under the soft glow of the candlelight. "I don't remember who the other messenger was," he lied, withholding the whole truth from her.

"Shaydin and Kadir came over the morning after you went looking for Talmage. Did you tell them both?"

"Shaydin isn't a messenger. He's too slow." Jaromir continued to lie.

"If you want us to make it out of here alive, Jar, you need to tell Pius."

Jaromir sighed, and his chest deflated like someone had stomped on him. "I don't think he'll let both of us out of here alive, even if I do tell him."

"Don't say that! We're both getting out of here." Zylah's words echoed across the small dark room.

The constant tapping of the blacksmith's anvil echoed outside. Jaromir rested his head back and noticed the vines climbing the wall above the well. Some of the slender stems held onto the ceiling like a hand clasping onto it. The stones were stained with swirls of misshapen patches of white and brown substances.

"Where do you think we are?" Zylah asked, breaking his thoughts.

"I'm not sure," Jaromir mumbled. "Maybe in the Shanty District, beyond the inner wall." *Pius wouldn't be that stupid to lock us up somewhere that was so easy to be found.*

"Why would we be here?" Her high-pitched voice was filled with panic. The chains rattled above her head.

"If I was interrogating, I'd take my captives to someplace no one knew, and no one could hear us. It's easier to discard dead bodies when there's no one around that cares about inner-city people. Hundreds of people die nearly every day in the Shanty District, but everyone in the center turns their back towards the truth of this world. We're a long way from home," Jaromir answered.

"We need to get home," Zylah sobbed. "Is there a way to escape?"

"There is, but it's a life-or-death risk. I'm not willing to put you in that situation. You've been through enough." Jaromir hated that she was involved. If she hadn't, he would've tried to lash out at Pius with no concern of the consequence, but he knew how interrogations panned out. The sorcerer was using Zylah to get him to disclose his strategy and schemes. "If we can rip the head from the snake, the body will die. We need to eradicate Pius."

"No one is going to save us. We need to save ourselves." Jaromir stared at Zylah's silhouette in the dim candlelight. She was suspended above the ground, hanging from the chains connected to the ceiling.

Jaromir noticed the candles had burned to half their size since being lit. The rope stretched to the ceiling along the candles' base and attached to it was a large iron ball. Jaromir studied it; he was puzzled by the mechanism above his wife's head. *Why would that be...* Suddenly, it became clear. "Zylah! Look above you." Jaromir shouted.

His heart began to beat fast and loud. Zylah turned her head, the wax cracking and crumbling off her, and observed the candle and rope. "I can't see it."

"When the candles finish burning, the rope around it will drop and pull the ball off the ledge, and it'll land on top of you!" Rage ran through his limbs.

Zylah began to panic, pulling on the chains around her wrists and ankles. "What do I do?"

Jaromir could hear her sobbing and rattling the chains. "It's going to be okay," he attempted to reassure her.

"How's it going to be okay?" She shouted back at him. "I have to get out of here!" She continued to thrash about.

Jaromir glanced around at his options to escape. He observed the chains wrapping around his wrists and ankles. They stretched to the rolling pins at either end of the wooden board he lay on. He wriggled his hands and attempted to pull them through, but the bottom of his palms was slightly wider and got stuck on the shackle. As Zylah tried to free herself, Jaromir persisted in removing his wrists. *I just need one.* Pulling down against the restraints and tucking his thumbs in to try to make them narrower. *Come on.*

The edge of the cuff dug into his skin; sharp pains pierced through his joints. He flinched at the agony but suppressed the pain. His palm slowly shrank as he pulled down. A loud crack popped from his wrist.

Jaromir bellowed in pain.

His palm half stuck in the shackle and throbbed against the cuff. He breathed slow through clenched teeth. The flame rested close to his ribs and sizzled his skin.

"What are you doing?" Zylah asked, her voice filled with concern.

"I'm trying to get… my hands out…" He answered, resuming his attempt to free his wrist.

Jaromir's thumb folded inward, the broken bones shifted and sent agonizing pain up his arm. He thrust his hand with one last effort, pulling his shoulder downwards. The pressure of the flat cuffs wrapped around his wrist and tightened.

He winced and screamed in pain. Slowly it slipped further down, until one last jolt of pain, Jaromir freed his hand. He was breathing deep and sweat ran his face. The excruciating pain throbbed in his wrist and hand. Jaromir pulled his arm down. The muscles around his shoulder were tight as he rested his wrist against his chest. He began to shiver in pain.

"Are you okay?" Zylah asked with a soft, sympathetic voice.

Jaromir took deep breaths. With each exhale, his shoulders jittered, and his wrist burned in pain. "I'm fine…" His eyelids grew heavy with each blink. Slowly, he began to give in to fatigue.

He shifted and moaned. The thought of breaking his joints tensed his insides. Conflicted with pain and freedom, he forced himself to stay awake.

"Jar, you can't do this to your body. You wouldn't be able to fight."

"I could save you," he mumbled, rolling his head towards her. Zylah's watery eyes glistened in the faint candlelight. Above her, the candle had nearly burned out.

She's right. I can't escape if everything's broken. "What happened to Kadir and Shaydin?" Jaromir asked his wife, thinking back on what Pius said before he left.

Zylah sniffed and cleared her throat. "You don't remember?"

"No, I don't," Jaromir lied.

"He and Shaydin infiltrated Pius' council and spied on his plans before they rode for Tahunan."

Had she been eavesdropping on us that night? Jaromir narrowed his gaze at her. "How do you know all of this?"

Zylah began to say something but stopped herself.

"How do you know about the order and our plans?" Jaromir demanded from her.

She remained silent.

"Tell me!" Jaromir lurched at her. His broken wrist sent sharp pains up his arm and through his neck. He winced and flopped back onto the table, breathing deeply, and wishing she hadn't told Pius about Kadir.

"We have to get out of here, Jar."

Jaromir glanced over at her. "I know we do. What about Kadir? He's caught up in all this because of you." *If Pius does have Kadir, where is Shaydin?*

"I don't give a shit about him or any of your men!" Zylah screamed. "We need to get out of here!"

Jaromir let her voice fade in the room. He hadn't been candid with her, but neither had she. Unexpected ventures for days at a time, visiting her family near The Cleave. *Did she see Talmage?* Jaromir brewed on her lack of honesty as he listened to her faint sobs.

All his thoughts ate away at him. Not only did the fact of how much his wife was lying to him but they were stuck together and Jaromir had no idea where his comrades were or if they were alive.

Zylah cleared her throat, interrupting his thoughts. Jaromir heard the solidified wax over her head crack at every movement she made in the corner.

"Pius said you told him something. What did you tell him?"

"I've already told you!" Zylah began to sob. "After you went looking for Talmage, Pius and his men ambushed me. Pius knew I had been speaking to your brother."

Jaromir's breath deepened, and his mouth was dry. He'd been sober since he took Agustin's life, but if an ale was given to him, he would gladly finish it. He glanced around in the dark, the candles above were three-quarters depleted, and the rope had shifted lower.

Zylah shuffled, her buckles rattled in the shadows of the wicked torture room. "My head hurts. The wax is ripping out my hair and pulling off my skin." Her voice was soft as if she had given up hope. "I want this to be over."

"I want this to be over as well." Jaromir held back his tears with shallow breaths.

The sound of Zylah shifting her body across the cobblestone floor and the wax crackling from her scalp filled the darkroom. She winced and whimpered with each movement.

TALMAGE

His feet stumbled over loose rocks, chasing after the dark figure disappearing down the passageway. He never saw Agustin after that moment. Talmage knew his brother was searching for Pius, but he had never known how Agustin had died. He was told by Jaromir it had been from natural causes. *That was the first time he hugged me since we were young.* Talmage collapsed and shouted into his hands. His cry faded into the shadows of the darkness. For a while, Talmage sat in silence on the cold ground. *Could Jaromir have killed him? Is he that loyal to his order?* He glanced at the humming soft light. He made his way back to the lake.

He kneeled and splashed his face. The body of water rippled with each handful he stole from it. He drank until his belly was full. An icy chill shivered down his spine as he examined the area around the lake. *It feels like I've been down here forever.*

Talmage splashed his face once more before following the vines to undo his brother's wrongs. He entered the dark opening past the lake, reflecting on his guardian's words. A fit of anger spawned within him. Pius had told him to watch and follow his brother, but he never managed to find Jaromir's headquarters, where he met with his associates. Talmage had always been left out of his brother's plans and life. It was the way it was. Agustin showed

Jaromir the swords' path and brute strength, whereas their guardian had given Talmage books and spells.

His short, fast breaths filtered around him. Talmage struggled to breathe as he weaved down the tunnels. The thought of dying in the light-starved maze became increasingly present in his situation. His wheezing cough strangled his throat as he ran. The shortness of his breath squeezed his chest, and he stopped and kneeled. Coughing into his damp shirt, his insides wrung and twisted. He couldn't stop it. His whole life, he had suffered from the condition.

After his convulsion, he leaned over, taking shallow breaths through his shirt. He stared at the soft glimmer from the moist vines. *How am I going to get out of here?* Talmage questioned himself.

"Is this necessary?" He bellowed, hoping Pius was watching or listening. "How will this prove that I'm to be the next ruler? I don't understand."

Nothing.

Talmage respected and idolized Pius. He had taught the young sorcerer more magick than Agustin or books could ever show him. As he frowned at the darkness, clenching his fist, his admiration morphed to hatred.

The deeper Talmage stumbled along the passages, the more the vines thinned up the walls around him. His vision adjusted to the shadows. Rocks crumbled under each footstep, and water drops echoed in the nothingness. A soft breath of air carried a scent of wet soil and grass. He held onto the vines as he stumbled through the passages.

Talmage was sick of forcing down the furry moss. His stomach growled for a hearty meal and a frothy ale at the Amalgamate. As he reflected on the tavern, a memory came before him. After a long winter day, he and Jaromir were sitting at the bar the day after Agustin had died. The tavern's fireplace drew the people from afar, filled with laughter and drunken stories. Jaromir sat close to Talmage at the bar. His smile stretched up his face. *That lying prick. He sat there knowing what he'd done.*

A hot flush rushed through Talmage's cheeks, and his heart pounded thumping against his ribs like a bird trying to escape from its cage. Talmage let out a shout of anger, trying to cast all his spells. One incantation after the other, throwing his hands out yelling into the passages but nothing. "Why did Jaromir have to kill him?" He leaned against the wall, his legs ached, and his throat was wheezy.

A soft slithering touch curled up his leg. He peered downwards to see vines climbing up his foot and ankle. Talmage kicked it off and crouched over to have a closer look. The vines slowly slithered closer, inch by inch. More tree limbs began to grow up his boot. As he jumped up, the plants around him started to climb the walls and smother the ceiling. Growing as fast as if they were hunting him, trying to consume him. The vine stalks flailed and swung off the surface. Talmage ducked and weaved through the passage as it closed in. The growth rate spread like a fire running through dry grass, bouncing, and grabbing anything it could reach. Talmage ran past his mark and fled into the dark passage.

The vines slithered and crumbled the rocks and walls. Talmage ran and stumbled on the loose and moving ground. Suddenly, a vine swung at him, splitting his tunic. More attacked him, increasing in size, and shifting fast like thick snakes. Talmage dodged and leaped over them. A limb clenched his foot and tripped him over. Before he could get up, another vine grabbed his leg. A thick vine dangled from the ceiling over him. Talmage stared at it. It contemplated him as if it had eyes peering at him.

The vines wrapped around his feet. Talmage stumbled over the vine as he reached for it. "Help me!" Talmage shouted out. "Bethany… Agustin." He grunted, squirming on the thick wet plants.

He pulled his foot free of his boots and crawled over piles of vines. Up ahead, he saw the two tunnels he followed before. The second opening was clear. Talmage kicked and shoved the slimy vines as other large vines swung at him, forcing him to the ground. He rolled over and placed out his hands.

"Ardeat ignis." He shouted.

Columns of fire exploded from his palms, incinerating the vines and scorching anything in his way. The plants flailed and thrashed about, trying to shake off the flames before turning to ash. The rolling flames traveled down the passage, snapping from his palms, and leaving him in darkness, panting and holding his hands out. A harsh sizzling blared from the lake as the fire extinguished. Talmage smiled and fell onto his back, taking deep breaths of smoke. Before he could enjoy his victory, his throat tightened, and he convulsed into a violent coughing attack.

He slowly stood, holding his tunic over his mouth, and making way for the opening to his left, away from the scorched vines.

JAROMIR

Jaromir fell in and out of sleep. He struggled to rest when he was chained against his will, tied down and stretched like an elastic band. His elbow and knee joints were weak, and the taste of blood remained in his mouth.

"Zylah, are you there?" Jaromir leaned over and peered at the corner.

Sott rustles of her chain jingled as she shuffled on the stone ground. Zylah cleared her throat. "I'm here, but I need help…"

Jaromir's body ached. He listened to the rhythmic tings of the blacksmith's anvil and sizzling iron coming from outside the room. He had hoped for an act of triumphant revenge on the sorcerer that took his parents. Since he was young, he had trained with the sword and dagger, eliminating his disciples, trying to reach the head of the snake, but as he lay in the confined prison, the fire of revenge burned fresh in his thoughts.

The heavy door flung open.

Jaromir threw his arm back above and pretended that it was chained. Two silhouettes stood in the doorframe. Jaromir recognized the outline of Pius and one of his giant brutes. They entered, slamming the door behind them. Pius held the flame out in front of him.

"It stinks in here. Morten, open the window and let out that stench of death."

"Sir, no window."

"Oh, my mistake, we did make sure of that, didn't we? At least your brother has the freshness of a cool breeze." Pius laughed. The flame dancing shadows on his face.

"Where's Talmage? You twisted bastard!" Jaromir wanted to leap and almost showed his free hand.

"The first rule of interrogation is to refrain from offending the captor. If you want to know where Talmage is, you need to tell me your grand scheme of suppressing us." Pius leaned over and held fire to his face. "All your men and the emperor's guards are hunting me down, interrogating my people, and soon…" Pius' voice trailed off, and he nodded at Morten.

Jaromir hadn't noticed where the brute was standing. He flicked his gaze and Morten held the pole. "No! Please don't!" He was close to spilling his plans, but trying to give it more time, just in case Shaydin, had ventured across The Cleave without him. As he begged, behind Pius, a silhouette stood over him. The outline held something high in the air. Jaromir peered past the sorcerer, but Pius noticed he was staring beyond him. Pius quickly turned around, swiveling the flame, and revealing Zylah holding a sickle above her head.

How did she get out of it? Jaromir watched as she struck down. Pius narrowly dodged her attack and grabbed Zylah by the throat. Morten's heavy footsteps rushed over as Pius strangled Zylah. He spun his head around and stared at his free hand.

"How did you free yourself? Didn't you tighten it up enough, half-wit?" Pius held out his hand, ready to cast fire at his servant. Morten cowered down like a dog prepared to receive another beating. The sorcerer ceased his flame as Zylah jerked and kicked him.

"Let go of her! Stop it!" Jaromir thrashed his body. He reached over to grab Pius' cloak with his broken hand, but he couldn't get a grip.

"Pitiful. Didn't you think that your hand would serve no purpose when it's broken? You truly are an antimagick soldier." Pius tightened his grip around Zylah's throat. She gargled in agony.

Jaromir lunged at him. No matter how hard he tried, the chains held him down, and his hands couldn't pull Pius away from his wife. The conjured flame sizzled Zylah's neck as he strangled her with his long thin fingers. Her neck was glowing red, and her throat boiled.

"What was your plan, Zylah? Cut me down and free your husband. How do you think you would've escaped from Morten?" Morten grabbed the woman by her shoulders, and Pius let go and brushed his hands. "I think I got some wax on me." Morten held Zylah above the ground.

"Now, what to do with you, woman." Pius observed the candle nearly burnt out, holding the rope. He glanced back at the flailing women before lighting up the torches hanging on the wall. Pius walked from one torch to the next and hummed a tune. Different tools hung on a wooden board; scissors, wooden wedges, a bulging waterskin, tongs, clamps, hammers, and other tools Jaromir had never seen before.

Zylah thrashed her wax-covered head around as Morten held her tight in his grip.

"Let go of her!" Jaromir demanded.

"We can't be doing that." Pius stood before the wall of tools, twisting his wiry beard. "I think this lady needs to be reminded that when held captive, you need to respect the captor for both parties to achieve their desired goal... Ah, this one." Pius grabbed the tongs and held the end over the torch.

"What are you doing? Leave her out of it. She has nothing to do with it. I was the one that sent the messages and rallied against you. Please don't hurt her anymore. Can't you see she's suffered enough!" Jaromir screamed and begged for his wife.

Zylah tried to kick the brute harder in the chest, but Morten stood firm like a stone wall.

"Oh, do you think they're for her?" Pius twisted the tongs in the faint light. "No, no, no. These are for you, dear friend." Pius pulled the tong from the flame and tapped his finger on it. It sizzled his fingertips, and he flapped his hand around. He continued, "It's unpleasant but, fortunately for me, it'll keep my hands clean." His thin smile stretched up his narrow cheeks.

Jaromir kicked and wriggled his body, convulsing and urging to break free. His arm flapped on the table, and he tried to sit up, but he had no strength. "Please don't, I won't tell anyone about you. Please, I'm begging for my wife and me!"

"You do not care for her!" Pius clenched his jaw and glared at her with his ominous black eyes.

"She's with a child!" He pleaded.

Pius stopped. He looked at Zylah. "She doesn't seem like it." He walked closer to her.

"She missed her bleeding." Jaromir continued the lie.

"Is it true?" The sorcerer glanced at the woman. Zylah nodded hesitantly. "Ah, this is wonderful. We should celebrate."

Pius turned around, hung the tongs back in their fixture, and grabbed the waterskin and wooden wedges. He popped the cork from the skin and took a sip. He walked closer to Jaromir. Jaromir's heart raced, and his breath quickened. The sorcerer sat on the wooden plank and took another sip from the skin. "The freshest wine from across The Cleave, with a sweet taste of berries and cracked pepper. Can you smell it?" He waved the mouthpiece under Jaromir's nose. Jaromir flicked his head away. "Go on, have a sniff. It's delicious," Pius persisted.

Jaromir stared at his beading dark eyes. His black hair shimmered with the orange glows from the torches scattered around the room. The wax had given shape to where Zylah endured her cruel torture. She looked at Jaromir. Her eyes were puffy and red, a thick layer of wax molded over her hair, with one long strand of resin covering half her face. Above her, the candle had almost burnt out.

Pius waved it under Jaromir's nose, and he hesitantly craned his neck closer. The spicy pepper stung his nostrils. Jaromir inhaled the scent, drawing a more profound scent–*the sweetness of blackberries*. Saliva formed and it reminded him of the wine that he hid beneath his house just in case he was ever tempted. The desire to have a sip was burning strong in his mind, but he made a promise to himself.

"Ah. You know your wine, don't you, Jaromir? The richest and finest spice for the Empress and her council." Pius took another sip. "Have you tried this before?"

Jaromir refused to answer him. The sorcerer had caused enormous amounts of pain to his wife, and only the gods know what he has done to Talmage.

Pius's jaw muscles bulged in the torchlight. He took another sip from the sack. "See, what frustrates me the most, is that I offer a celebratory refreshment for this child, coming into this forsaken world, and you lie to my face!" His voice grew into a loud bellow, echoing from the walls. He stood up and glared down at him. "I know you have tasted this wine. It was at your house. Don't you think I've scoured your place for all your plans?" He straightened his robe. "Maybe I let my guard down. I tried to reason with you, and you chose to withhold the truth!" Pius looked at Morten and waved him towards Jaromir.

Jaromir glanced at Morten pacing over, his heavy steps thudding on the stone floor. The servant grabbed his head. He tossed about, trying to pull his head from Morten's grip. Morten held his head like a vice grip and opened his mouth.

Jaromir tried to close it, feeling the pain streak through his jawbone as if it was about to snap off. Zylah was screaming and shouting at them to stop and leave him alone.

"'I'll burn this city down if I must, Jaromir, with you and your wife. I know she's not with a child. I'm not a fool! I'm past the point of trying to reason with you. You've lied to me. You know where you sent your other messengers. If your alliances are expecting a reply from Kadir, it shall be forgotten. His fate has been intertwined with your brothers."

"What have you done with them?"

Pius pried his jaw open. "Don't worry—Talmage has Kadir's life in his hands."

Jaromir thrashed about, but it was too late. The sorcerer leaned over and flowed the wine into his mouth. At first, Jaromir tried to swallow each mouthful as Pius poured more wine into his mouth. It filled his nose and spilled down his face. Jaromir violently coughed the wine out of his mouth, his throat tensing and tongue swelling, yet the sorcerer continued to gush it into his mouth. The sweet blackberries were cloying his throat, and the sharp pepper stung his nostrils. He tried to flick his head away from the waterfall of wine, choking him. Morten held his head, and Pius stopped the flow of liquid. Jaromir coughed and spat the blood-colored wine. Morten let go and he spewed the wine on the wooden plank. It splashed onto the ground. Taking deep breaths in between his stomach bowels, rejecting the volumes of wine poured down his throat. Long strands of stained spit and mucus hung from his stubble beard.

"Don't fucking lie to me again, or you won't take another breath." Pius tossed the empty wineskin across the ground.

Morten's face glanced down at him with sorrow-filled eyes. He grabbed the rag and cleaned Jaromir's face. At first, Jaromir avoided the cloth, taking in deep breaths, but Morten seized his head and wiped his face with his large calloused hands.

"What are you doing?" Pius pulled Morten off him.

"Cleaning." His voice was slow and deep, as if he spoke another language outside of The Three Kingdoms. Jaromir stared into the brute's eyes. They were icy blue like the sky on a clear day.

The sorcerer conjured a flaming violet chain and wrapped it around Morten's throat. Morten fell to the ground, detaching the keys from his belt. The slid across the ground. Pius and Morten hadn't noticed and Jaromir resisted the urge to glance at his chance of freedom. Pius dragged his servant out around the neck, Morten choking and gasping for air, also leaving the torches lit and the rag on Jaromir's wrist.

The stone door slammed closed behind his captors. Jaromir waited for the coast to be clear, their footsteps fading up the hallway. As soon as he deemed it safe, he grabbed the wet cloth with his broken hand. Moving it with his hand, but sharp pains ran through his forearm. He cried in pain.

"Why are you trying to use the rag?" Zylah asked, leaning towards him.

Jaromir couldn't look at her grotesque face. "If I can somehow wedge it under the cuffs, it might be wet enough to slip me out of this prison." Jaromir shifted onto his hip and used his arm to slide the rag up to his other wrist.

"What happens if it doesn't work?" Zylah asked with a tone of doubt.

He used all his force to shift the rag, focusing on the task at hand, not on his wife's question.

"Jar, what then?" she persisted.

"I don't know!" He shouted at her. "I can't give up now. I can't give up on you or Talmage." Jaromir looked at her. Instead of anger building in him, a sense of sadness pressed on him. Her face reflected the glowing torches. A yellow tinge molded to her scalp and solidified over her face. Jaromir felt tears forming. He squeezed his eyelids tight, pushing the tears away. Even though she had betrayed him, the sight of his wife's predicament took away the role of being her husband. A protector and a guardian from anyone that would cause her harm, like Agustin was to him and his brother. She was strong enough to take care of herself, but he had always felt the need to protect her—but he failed her.

"I'm sorry, Zyl." He cleared his throat. His wrists and ankles burned with each movement, and his muscles were stretched out like an animal hide.

"Don't be sorry. It's not your fault."

"It is my fault! If I didn't ask Kadir and Shaydin to leave, we wouldn't be here. If I hadn't devoted my life to hunt down Pius, we wouldn't be here!" Jaromir took deep breaths. He had blurted out his secret. He turned to his wife. Zylah stared at him with dark circles looped down her face.

Jaromir rested his head back on the wood. He wiggled his toes and fingers to keep the blood circulating. He sighed. *Why are the gods so cruel?*

An inner turmoil circulated in his thoughts. On the one hand, he was biding his time for his reinforcements, but it was his dear friends. "I don't know what to do. My right could be someone else's wrong—and that someone else is, Kadir or Shaydin."

"What do you think he'll do to them?"

"Probably worse than what he's done to us." The taste of pepper lingered on Jaromir's lips.

"Can you trust them?"

Jaromir thought about it for a while. Kadir was a quiet man but ruthless on the battlefield. Jaromir had seen him annihilate sorcerers more times than he could count. In contrast, Shaydin was the loudest and proudest of the two comrades. "With my life," Jaromir finally answered.

"It's your choice, Jar, but I don't think Pius is a man of reason. He'll do anything to you, me, or Talmage to get what he wants."

"I think I know a way out of here." Jaromir began pushing the rag up towards his wrist, shifting his limb, tossing it, and rolling it closer towards his hand. With one final shove, it tumbled within reach, and he grabbed it.

"Yes!" Zylah gasped.

I don't even know if this will work, but it's worth a shot. Jaromir tried to slip the wet rag into the chain, slithering it down, but it wouldn't go in. Sweat beads dripped down his face, and his breathing deepened. *Come on.* Jaromir shoved the rag down between the skin and chain. He suppressed the pain running up his arm as he finally forced the material through the cuff. He pulled the wet rag, from the other side and wriggled it free. The cool breeze from the crack under the door tickled his exposed skin. His broken wrist had a bit of strength but not enough to wield a weapon.

The feeling of freedom smothered him.

Jaromir took deep breaths and studied his free arms. *I'm free.*

"Quickly!" Zylah urged him.

He returned to his task and leaned over the table edge. The chains had a little slack in them, enough for him to get off the table and reach for the keys on the ground. He slid off. As he put pressure on his feet, he realized his legs were weak, as if he was asleep for days. He shuffled along the cold ground and grabbed the keys.

Jaromir bent over and unlocked the chains. The heavyweight fell from his ankles.

"Yes!" Zylah shouted. "Quickly, come over and get me out of here."

Jaromir rushed over to her. As he kneeled in front of her, the wax glimmered in the torchlight. He fumbled through the keys, trying each one on the leather vest and the chains around her wrists, but none of them fit. "Shit!"

"What is it?" Zylah tilted her head towards him.

Jaromir stood and pulled on the chains. "None of the keys fit."

"Are you serious?" Desperation crackled in Zylah's voice.

He remembered the set of keys jingling on Morten's waist. "The keys aren't here."

Zylah pulled rattled the chains, trying to break them. Jaromir helped her, but it proved useless.

"Renold must have the keys." Jaromir lowered himself to eye level. Her eyes watered, and the wax reflected the flickering candle lights. She was taking in deep breaths.

"I forgive you, Zylah, and I'm sorry for neglecting you for so long. We're both going to escape from here. I promise." He kissed her warm cheek and stood up.

"I'm sorry, Jar, but please, you can't leave me here by myself!"

"There's no other way. I have to go before they come back." Jaromir went to the wall with the assorted tools on them and grabbed the small sickle. "I'll be back for you, I promise." He opened the door and walked into the dark hallway.

TALMAGE

Talmage stumbled through the passages. The spell had depleted his energy. *The curse of magick.* After each spell, it would drain the user, but Talmage had put everything he had into his last spell. Now he paid the consequences of his life-saving actions.

Why could I use it then and not before? He wondered, staring at his black-singed palms. He glanced around, wondering if his mentor had been watching him and allowed him to use his magick. His dry, cracked lips burned in the cold air as he staggered absently down the passage.

"Hello!" His frail voice faded in the distance, hoping someone had entered the warded labyrinth. *I've got to... keep... going.*

Talmage made his way through the passages, attempting to retrace his steps from following his ex-lover. As he paced through the system of black openings and narrow walls, he struggled to remember his last thoughts before waking up in the caves. He thought of his brother and wondered if he was in the same predicament as him. *Probably not, his life had been blessed with greatness——climbing the ranks of the Empress' Military while I climbed over foes in the shadows.* He saw his brother less often after Agustin had died. Zylah had always been kind to him and wrote him letters in secrecy. Her last letter had hurt him the most, but maybe it was something he needed to receive.

Tal.

Jaromir nearly found your last letter, by the stovetops. Luckily, he can't read otherwise... We have been doing this for years, but I think it's time to stop this and come out and tell your brother your secrets. He needs to know, and I'm sure he'll still love you. You need him, and as much as he refuses to believe, he'll need you one to save his life.

In the last few months, Jar has become more obsessed with finding the sorcerer that killed your parents. Day and night, he spends roaming the city and outside the walls. Even when he's home, he hardly speaks to me, but I can't leave him. This will be my last letter. I'm sorry but take care of yourself, Tal.

Love always, Zy.

Talmage rubbed his head at the memory of the letter. *Maybe I deserve this.* Talmage sighed and continued walking through the darkness. *Would Jaromir murder him? Is this all a game to get rid of Jaromir? Jaromir...* Talmage squeezed his black-singed palm.

Thinking his brother infuriated him. Since that fateful day where he discovered his greatest strength and killed his parents, only Agustin filled that void but no matter how many ales he drunk, the memory of the fire burned in his consciousness.

After a while, and feeling slightly restored after using his spell, he called out. "Is anyone in here?"

Talmage stopped and pressed both his hands on the wall. Sweat dripped down his face, and the cold air tightened his throat. Suddenly, Talmage fell into a wheezing cough. His lungs compressed, and his throat wheezed. Each cough burned his throat and dried his mouth. He fell to the ground, his limbs were weak, and his head throbbed. He caressed his wispy brown hair and spat on the floor. *I don't think I'll ever make it out.* He had finally given up hope of escaping; it was his fate to die alone, to pay for his sinful way of life and become a ghost of his past.

"Hello?" A voice echoed down from the darkness.

I'm starting to hear voices. Talmage used the wall to stand up. He stared down at the darkness.

"Is anyone there?" The voice came again.

Talmage's heart dropped, and he flicked his head towards the voice. *Is it another ghost?* He nervously strolled towards the voice. "Who is it?" He stumbled through the dark passages, towards the voice.

His voice reverberated along the tunnel. His heart fluttered and his hot breaths floated behind him. It was an absurd thought, but...

"Jaromir?"

Even though Talmage held resentment against Jaromir for all the wicked things he had done, thinking of his twin brother wandering around the dark caverns could help him escape and keep him sane.

Talmage called out. "Jaromir?"

"It's not Jaromir." A male voice finally replied. It was louder as if Talmage could reach out and touch it.

He stopped in his tracks. "Who is it then?" He waited for the voice to reply. The sound of his heartbeat loud and his shallow breaths filled the cave. He looked at his palm. *I can't use my magick, and I can't fight.*

The tunnels were dead. The bitter taste of metal lingered, and a faint smell of moist dirt hung in the air.

Not often had he felt fear or doubt, especially through Pius's trials to learn the art of magick but the unknown voice made him question his next action. Talmage hoped it was someone he knew and could overpower them if things got complicated.

The voice paused for a while. Talmage held his breath, trying to stay as quiet as possible, waiting for him to reply, with his fists clenched. As Talmage was about to shout out, the voice answered.

"I'm not sure."

It's not Jaromir. "Do you have a weapon?"

"I don't think so." Shifting noises came from the tunnel.

"Stay where you are."

Talmage crept through, hesitantly towards the man. Cautious of him hiding and ready to attack him but as he emerged from a corner, caressing his hand along the wall. His fingers fell into a groove in the wall, and he felt a vertical indent. Talmage stopped and peered closer at the carved outline. It was the 'T' engravement.

A wave of frustration tensed through his arms. *I'm back where I woke up. Did I go around in circles?* He looked around at the openings that Bethany had led him towards the lake and, along with the vines, in a roundabout way to bring him back to the beginning, where he woke up.

"Where are you?" Talmage's voice trailed off down the passages. Questions ran through his mind. Had he been there the whole time? Did they get thrown in together? Maybe he knows who put them in here and if Jaromir is stuck in there with them.

"I'm here. Who's there?"

"It's Talmage!" He bolted towards the male's voice. A cool breeze swept past his ankles, and a sense of excitement rushed through his body. It was his first breakthrough of escaping the dark tunnels and his loneliness.

"Did you put me down here?" The husky male voice asked.

Talmage stopped and scrunched his face in confusion. "I'm stuck here too. Are you hurt?" As he crept closer along the narrow passageways, Talmage noticed a soft light glistening along the walls.

The man remained silent.

"Are you there?" Talmage shouted. The voice didn't respond. Talmage began to pace, suppressing the daunting thoughts of the continued loneliness in the labyrinth.

JAROMIR

Jaromir crept out of the room. The arch hallway extended into the distance. Faint whooshes of the blacksmith reverberated around him. He trod lightly along the cold stone ground, holding the sickle in front of him, and wary of any danger to jump out at him. He listened for any noises further ahead.

As Jaromir continued, his broken wrist tingled, and his hand that held the weapon trembled. His senses had failed him once before. *It's how I ended up in this shit hole. That sorcerer distracted me in the rain. Never again will they fail me.*

After a few paces, he glanced behind him to make sure no one followed. Jaromir had been a calculated soldier. Detached from his emotions that affected his outcome, but as he lurked in the stone hallway, to search for the keys, save his wife, and escape—he quivered. It wasn't the first time he had so many of his allies rely on him, but nothing about his current situation had been planned. Not on his behalf.

A faint jingle came from up ahead.

Jaromir pressed his back to the side of the hallway. His heart raced, and he quietened his breaths. Waiting a few moments before continuing, listening for anyone or anything. Nothing appeared. It was clear. He followed the windy hallway until it finally came to an end. Another door stood before him—a wooden door with a window with four iron bars in the middle of it.

Jaromir slid to the wall. He could hear a soft wheezy breath and someone sniffing their nose. He peeped through the opening. Renold sat on a chair in a sizable empty room. It was dimly lit by candles with pockets of darkness. The large brute sat next to the door with his thick arms folded in a musky gray tunic, and a leather belt with a mace hanging off it. Around his neck, a gold chain with an emerald jewel rested on his chest. Renold moved, and the keys hung off the back of his belt. Jaromir sank back from view, hearing the keys jingle with the brute's movements.

How am I going to get them? Jaromir looked around at his options. He peeked into the door opening.

Renold was gone.

Jaromir searched the room. He saw another door at the far end, and in front of it, Renold stood.

I don't have a choice. Jaromir put his hand on the cold metal door handle. His wrist shivered from pain, and it was useless in battle. He held the sickle and readied his grip. *Everyone is counting on me like always.*

Jaromir twisted the door handle and flung the door open. Renold turned around and glared at him.

"How did you get out?" Renold asked, his voice deep and slow-witted.

Jaromir smiled, analyzing his opponent. *This'll be easy.* "It wasn't too hard with the keys."

"How did you get them off Morten? He left with Master." Renold moved closer to him.

"I guess he forgot to check before he left the room." Jaromir shifted his body weight to his back foot. "When I first met you, I had a feeling I'd have to kill you to escape."

Renold's hairless face crinkled as he grinned. "So did I."

The large brute moved across the room. Jaromir frowned at how soft his feet moved across the ground. Before Jaromir had time to plan his attack, Renold stood in front of him.

Renold had withdrawn his mace and swung it at Jaromir. Jaromir jumped back, dodging the swipe, followed by another swing. Renold reached to grab him, but Jaromir shoved the thick arm to the side, evading the hand, and countered with a slice across Renold's left thigh.

The brute bellowed. Jaromir jumped back and readied his stance. *He's more alert than Morten.* Renold wiped the wound with his hand and flicked the blood to the side. He stood up straight and held his mace above his head.

They both anticipated for another attack. Jaromir had always waited for the first strike. It was what he had always done in his training sessions, especially with Agustin. Renold swung the mace down on him. Jaromir shifted to the side, narrowing his body before digging the sickle into Renold's shoulder. He pulled the blade out before Renold's hand could reach him. He dodged and ripped the blade behind the large man's leg, sending Renold onto his back. Blood pooled onto the ground as Renold shrieked in agony.

Jaromir sliced Renold's arm off that held the mace. Splatters of blood sprayed across the ground. Renold howled like a dying bear.

"It isn't fair. You helped Pius torture me, but that was too easy for you." Jaromir stood over him, staring down at the disfigured limb. Renold squirmed. His brute strength that Jaromir had seen the entire time he was imprisoned faded. Renold's broad chest took deep, slow breaths.

"You didn't put up much of a fight against a wounded man. Have you heard that saying?" Jaromir lifted his arm and studied his broken wrist. He crouched down next to Renold's troll-like head. Blood had swirled underneath the brute's body, and his breath had nearly stopped. "Beware of the injured soldier."

A sideswipe took out Jaromir's legs, dropping his weapon. Renold sat up and grabbed Jaromir's throat. Jaromir clawed at the brute's hand as it squeezed tighter, stealing his breath, and clamping his neck.

"I've heard that saying." Renold spat at Jaromir with blood-stained teeth. "Never let your guard down." As Renold leaned into Jaromir, a necklace flopped out of his tunic.

Each second, the brute's clasp strangled Jaromir. He reached for Renold's head, but his arms were too short. Pressure squeezed to behind his eyes. Jaromir dug his finger into Renold's hand, trying to break off the grip.

Renold drove his body into Jaromir, forcing him to the ground. He sat on top of him, putting his heavy body weight onto Jaromir's neck. "You know how to fight, but your ego and confidence was your downfall."

The necklace dangled in front of Jaromir. With his last ounce of energy, Jaromir grabbed the emerald jewel and pulled Renold's head close enough to dig his fingers into the brute's eye. Blood and pus squirted from his fingertips, gushing down his cheeks. Renold moaned and rolled off Jaromir.

He coughed and took a gasp of air. *It's not over yet.* He thought, clamming to his feet. Renold was losing a lot of blood, but to Jaromir's surprise, the brute was still alive. Jaromir stumbled to the mace and turned around.

Renold leaped at him. He swung the mace into his jaw, sending Renold down. Jaromir rose the mace above his head. Renold turned towards Jaromir. His eyes were bloody sockets with streams of red tears running down his cheeks, staining his tunic. The emerald necklace mirrored the candlelight like Talmage's eyes.

Jaromir had killed many people in his life, but as he stared down at the submissive brute, he hesitated for the life he was about to take. "I need to save everyone," he mumbled as he struck Renold's jaw.

It cracked and twisted Renold's neck. Sending the body to the ground. His breath had stopped, and blood seeped further away from the lifeless body. Jaromir dropped the weapon and collapsed. His throat wheezed like his brother's cough, and his arms burned with pain. He yearned to curl up and sleep off the pain. *I can't stop now. Not yet.*

Jaromir lifted his neck and looked at the dead body. Blood splattered onto the glistening emerald necklace. He leaned over, took the keys from his waist, and ripped off the necklace from Renold's neck.

A radiating warmth melted into his hand. He examined the ornament. It gave off a warm sensation, tingling up his arm and across his chest. Jaromir pulled the necklace closer for inspection. An intricate pattern of three flames and a circle was welded across it. He rubbed the back's rounded surface. The pain from his broken wrist ceased. As he scratched the smooth face, his blood-stained fingertips shivered.

Jaromir took deep breaths. *Is this magick?*

Twisting and observing it in the faint light. Glancing back and forth between the necklace and his wrist, an overwhelming temptation to use it and heal it came upon Jaromir. Sweat dripped down his jawline as the overpowering urge to use the magick to heal him. The thing that took everything and balanced the scales of life and death for his wife and brother. *I can't betray my parents and the order.* Jaromir shook away the thought and shoved the necklace into his pocket. It hummed a slight warmth, but it was bearable. The pain in his wrist poured back into his limb. He squeezed his teeth tight and staggered to the other door.

From behind him, a piercing scream came from the hallway.

Zylah. "I'm coming for you." Without thought, Jaromir marched to the door, swung it open, and back down the arch corridor.

Suddenly, a hand from the darkness grabbed Jaromir's wrist, and a burning pain raced up his arm. He turned to see who held him, but it was too dark and his vision blurred.

Jaromir wrestled, with the strange grabbing his wrist. Swinging his other hand at the unknown person but missed. The stranger grunted and grasped Jaromir's neck and thrust him to the ground. He gave into the overwhelming strength and the man dragged him back down the hallway.

TALMAGE

Talmage scrambled through his thoughts as he weaved in the darkness. The faint light reflecting off the wall filled the passageway around him. Talmage ceased rubbing his hands along the wall, following the cool breeze and the hoarse male voice. The words lingered like his first magick wound. It was when he and Pius were sparring. Pius had used the hastam glacies, spell, and sliced his skin, forever leaving a blue scar down his forearm. *Jaromir has the same scar, I wonder if he got it the same way.* He rubbed the scar and shuffled through the tunnels after the voice.

"Are you still there?" Talmage shouted.

Grunts and moans echoed down the passage.

"Stay there. I'm coming!"

As he turned around a corner, he came across a figure on the ground. The light lingered beyond the curves and turned past him. A harsher and icier breeze snapped across Talmage's skin, tingling his scar, and raising his arm hair.

Talmage hesitantly approached him, cautious of the figure being another ghost of his past. As he drew near, he realized it wasn't anyone he instantly recognized. With a sigh of relief, Talmage fell to the stranger's side. The discovery of someone else, a real person, brought tears to his eyes in the labyrinth prison. He sobbed and crawled to the man's side and placed his hand on his slumped shoulders. The last time he had cried was when Agustin had died. *Murdered*. He remembered, wiping his tears off his cheeks, and gathering himself. The man was taking shallow breaths and stunk of a long night on the ale. The smell made Talmage thirsty but he suppressed the urge.

"Are you hurt?" Talmage asked, looking over the stranger's body.

"I'll be fine. At least I'm not alone anymore." The man smiled at him.

Talmage shifted closer and peered at him. "Kadir?" It was the last person Talmage suspected to be put in the labyrinth prison with him. Jaromir's closest companion and his messenger.

"Are you okay? How did you get down here?" Talmage peered at the soldier. Questions flooded into his mind about his brother and if there was an exit. Kadir was wounded and exhausted.

Kadir's long disheveled hair hung on his shoulders. He wore a battered, long-sleeved shirt, and his pants were ripped with stains of blood and dirt. Kadir peered at Talmage with suspicion and confusion. "Jaromir?"

Talmage shook his head. "Close, but no, it's Talmage."

Kadir mumbled, rubbing his temple. "I once knew a Talmage. A young fellow with the world between his ears, great at climbing but useless with a weapon." He chuckled, turning to a slow cough.

Talmage blushed, even though Kadir couldn't see it. "It's me, remember?" He leaned his face closer.

"I see it is." Kadir briefly looked at him, his eyes rolled, and he broke into a coughing fit.

"Here, have this." Talmage wrung his damp shirt onto his lips, and it soothed his throat slightly to stop the heaving.

Kadir's cough ceased, and he leaned against the jagged rock wall. Beyond him, the passage gave off a dim light, different to the vines but a white light as if someone held a bright beacon. Talmage pulled out some of the edible moss and offered it to him. "It's not a hot roast, but it'll keep you going. How did you get here?" he asked, lifting Kadir's linen pants from the ankle to look for any apparent wounds. A few scrapes stretched around his lower leg and knees, but nothing crucial.

Kadir hesitantly accepted the moss and put a small amount into his mouth and chewed. "I don't know..."

"What happened to you?"

"The last thing I remember was trying to leave Valenor."

"Why were you trying to leave?"

Kadir peered at him then sighed. "How much do you know of your brother?"

More than he thinks. Talmage nodded.

"I'm not sure I'm the one that should be telling you." Kadir broke into another coughing fit, his throat swelling, and the rasping coughs reverberated off the shimmering walls. Talmage offered his shirt to ease the pain. Kadir took deep breaths and winced. "He ordered Shaydin and me to send a message to the other kingdoms."

None of it made sense, but Talmage understood it had something to do with his secrets. "What was the message?"

"To form an alliance against the sorcerer, Pius, and his disciples."

"Why are you telling me this?"

"Because you're his brother, and you need to know this."

Talmage felt his heart throbbing in his chest and his hands clenching. His anger for Jaromir evolved. *First, he kills Agustin, and now he wants to fight against Pius.* At that point, he wished he could conjure magick to prove Jaromir's primitive way was inferior, but Talmage closed his eyes and controlled his breaths.

"For years, we've been trying to rid the world of sorcerers, but I think Jaromir believes Pius is training someone to take his place."

Talmage wanted to tell him, but he promised Pius that he couldn't tell anyone about his mastery of magick. "Did Jaromir tell you why he loathes all magick users?"

"Magick burned your parents."

"That's some of the truth. It did burn our parents. Jaromir blames Pius for the fire, but the truth is, I did it. For some unexplainable reason, I was able to cast a spell. I've lived with the guilt my whole life. Jaromir has forged his whole life around his hatred for sorcerers, but in truth, he should hate me."

"You're lying."

"I wanted to tell Jaromir, but I know he'd never listen to me."

A soft icy breeze floated through the dark passage, giving Talmage goose pimples up his spine. The memory of the thunderous crack of lightning that struck the woods surrounding Tarnsby haunted his dreams. Talmage was only eight, and he was searching in the forest for a goat that had gone astray. The storm rolled out as fast as it came in, causing havoc, lightning, and fire. It was gone. Talmage had been trapped by burning logs, smoke-filled his breaths, and his vision faded. Suddenly, a deep inner rage took over his body, shooting a force field to expand and explode the wood. With his last ounce of life, he limped back to the village. As he crawled over the hill, he saw homes squashed and engulfed by the burning logs. He rolled down the mountain and saw everything ablaze.

Near their home, Jaromir hunched over two bodies. Talmage rushed to his side, and it was their parents. Limbs broken and scorched chests. Talmage wanted to tell Jaromir, but he couldn't. Talmage even tried to lie and blame the storm, but skies were filled with black smoke. Jaromir didn't believe him.

Kadir's wheezing breaths filled the silence of the tunnels, breaking Talmage's thoughts. He suppressed the scenes and cries of his brother and offered moss to Kadir, but he refused. Instead, Talmage took a bite of the dense and furry plant, then let out a deep sigh. "We need to get out of here."

"Where are we?" Kadir looked around him.

"I'm not sure. I went further ahead, and it led me to an underground lake but then it eventually led me back here. We should find where that breeze is coming from. Maybe that's an opening." Talmage stood and glanced in the direction he appeared from the depths of the labyrinth.

"Let's get some water." Kadir breathed heavily.

Talmage remembered his ghosts haunting him. "No, we can't. It'll take too long. The end might be close."

Kadir sighed. "How long have you been here for?"

"Maybe two or three days. I'm not sure."

"I can't die here."

"Now that we have each other, I think it'll be easier to stay sane and escape." Talmage crouched down and reassured him. Even though Kadir was one of Jaromir's Brother-In-Arms and despised their reasons for murdering his kind, Talmage needed him to survive. "We have more of a chance to get out of here now. We aren't alone anymore. Let's head this way." Talmage scooped him up under his arms and lifted him up. Kadir let out a shout of pain, tensing his torso and shoulders.

"What's wrong?" Talmage scanned the front of his body; he couldn't see any visible injuries.

"It's my back," Kadir answered with a weak voice.

Talmage lifted his arm up and turned him around. Across his back, a wide gash ran from his shoulders, across his spine, and to his tailbone. Blood seeped out, and the wound stuck to his stained shirt. Talmage hovered his hand over it and tried to cast a conjuration to heal it, but the feeling of a heavy glove weighed down on his arm. He scoffed. *Why isn't it working now?*

"What happened?" Talmage asked "Why didn't you say anything before?" Talmage turned him around.

Kadir's face was pale, his lips cracked, and gaze swayed absently.

"Hey. Hey!" Talmage tapped him on his face. "We'll get this cleaned." Talmage rested him on the ground and ripped his shirt off. The shirt peeled from his wound, ripping off layers of skin, causing it to bleed again. "We'll head to the lake and clean it out." As Talmage stared at it, an eerie feeling shivered across his scar. He didn't want to go back that way, but it seemed he had no choice.

Talmage pressed the shirt on the roof and absorbed the moisture onto it. He crouched over and dabbed the shirt over Kadir's face.

Kadir frowned at him. His dark eyes peered in the soft light, showcasing the patchy beard down his jawline. "No… this way…"

Talmage leaned him down and gently pulled off the shirt stuck to his wound. It split and blood oozed out like hot molten lava from a fissure. "We have to clean this or we won't make it out."

Kadir nodded and attempted to stand up, ready to move towards the cold breeze flowing into the tunnels. "We don't need to make it out, just you."

"I can't let you die in here." Talmage helped him stand. "We're both getting out of here. Alive."

Kadir grunted and shifted his tired body on Talmage's shoulder. They both limped towards the source of the cold breeze without saying another word. Talmage wanted to use his magick to heal Kadir's wounds, and several times he tried, but nothing happened. The scraping sound of Kadir's feet was swept away by the gentle wind, deeper and further into the labyrinth prison behind them. Talmage pressed the shirt against Kadir's wound with his free hand. "How's it feeling?"

Kadir shuffled his legs and cleared his throat. "It's okay. How did we get down here?"

"I know who brought us down here, but I don't know how you got down here."

"Who was it?" Kadir glanced at him. His face was weathered and pale.

"It was Pius."

"How do you know that?"

Talmage adjusted Kadir's weight on his shoulder. "His face is the last thing I remember before waking up in this shit hole," he lied.

He thought of the ghosts that had lingered with him in the caves. His ex-lover and his ex-mentor. Both dead. Both were taken too early, and he never got to say his goodbyes. He thought maybe Kadir was one of his ghosts at times, but he could feel his hot breath and smell the rotten flesh. He was as alive as he was.

He lifted his shirt. Peeling it from his skin, Kadir winced and cringed at the material, stripping off his back like molded wax from the skin. "You don't remember how this happened?" Talmage asked, inspecting the infected laceration. It had stopped bleeding. The edges of the gash had turned a deep red with chunks of fabric sticking in it. Talmage leaned closer and smelt it. It reeked of spoiled meat. "You need to get this stitched up." Talmage placed the shirt back on it. It was too stained with blood for him to put on. *I can't heal this.* Talmage put his hand over the wound with a last effort and softly chanted a healing incantation, so Kadir didn't hear it. It failed.

"I feel weak," Kadir said, attempting to move his head.

Talmage observed his pale face, and his lips had large cracks. "Let's keep going, before it's too late."

Kadir wobbled on his feet as Talmage tried to continue through the passageway. "Come on, at least try to walk."

"I... can't..." Kadir's breath was soft and husky.

"It's not like you haven't done this before." Talmage urged him.

The two men walked towards the soft light, the breeze tingling Talmage's exposed body. His chest hairs rose, and his back shivered with the fresh air.

Kadir looked at him and smiled.

"Have you had any word from your wife?" Talmage tried to distract him from their difficult circumstance.

The injured man waved his hand.

Talmage adjusted his shoulders under Kadir's arms. "Asa is a beautiful lady. Quite exotic. Is she from somewhere outside Esterford?"

"Asa… yes… from Armagh."

Talmage smiled. "Think of her, Kadir. You have to make it back to Asa, and I have to make it to Jaromir."

"Where's… Jaromir?"

"I'm not sure, but I hope he's not in here."

As he thought of Jaromir, his throat tightened. Even though they were the same age, Jaromir spoke down to him like an older brother or a disappointed father. Agustin had taken care of them after his parents died, and Jaromir had always made sure he was listening to Agustin. Talmage knew being a merchant was a cover for his sorcerous ways; not many had known Agustin's truth, only Talmage and Pius. *Somehow, Jaromir must have discovered it.*

Talmage stared at the soft light, and his eyes began to sting. Kadir winced in pain as he struggled to walk.

"We'll rest soon, but let's make it a little further. I know you can do it, Kadir."

Why is he here? Talmage pondered on the question, struggling to drag the wounded man. His arms and thighs burned, and his throat itched. *If this is about me being here, why is he here? Is it a test to save him? Or is Pius as wicked and merciless as he was when he was ruler?* The questions ran through Talmage's mind as they reached a bend that welcomed them with a bright light.

Talmage peered at it with suspicion.

A faint haze concealed what lay beyond. He struggled to focus, and his vision blurred. He squinted at the tunnel. His legs ached, and his shoulders burned under Kadir's extra weight. He looked at the wounded man, his eyes slowly closed, and his head tilted downwards.

"Kadir." Talmage shook his arms, trying to wake him up. Kadir's head rolled forward, and his face reflected the light. Talmage leaned over to place him down, but he lost his balance, swayed to the wall, dropped Kadir, and smacked his shoulders into the wall before hitting the ground.

Talmage grimaced in pain. He saw Kadir lying unconscious. Talmage crawled towards him. His throat tickled, and he grunted to cease it, but it flared. He broke into a deep cough. It twisted his intestines, closing his throat tightly. The pressure intensified around his head, throbbing at his temples. His throat felt as if razors sliced his insides. Talmage had a violent fit, and at small intervals, he gasped for air while Kadir lay beside him—unmoved by the loud convulsions.

Talmage crawled towards him. "Wake… up!" He struggled to shake him, in-between his coughing attack. Kadir's head rolled to the side.

Kadir lay motionless. Talmage grabbed his shoulders. "Wake up!" He shook him. He needed to save him and make it out of the labyrinth prison. *Together.* "Please, Kadir."

Talmage knew a spell that could bring the dead back; it was seldom used and consumed the user's life. When Agustin passed, Talmage had hovered over his body, contemplating sacrificing himself, but the courage never stirred within him. Instead, Jaromir had pressed his fingers against Agustin's neck for a pulse and a breath from his nose. *He was there.* Talmage suddenly realized. *It's true.* Suppressing the thought for the time, Talmage mimicked his brother and quickly put his palm under Kadir's nose. He placed his fingers on Kadir's neck. Nothing.

"Shit! Where did he put it?" Talmage pressed his fingers on the front of his neck. Nothing. Close to his jaw. Nothing. "Where the hell is it?" He shouted, frustrated and his dry throat burned.

Please don't do this to me. "You're not dying on my Kadir! I can't let you leave me!"

Without thought, he placed one hand on his chest, the other over Kadir's heart and chanted the resurrection spell. The heavy gloves of the magick ward squeezed his hands and pressed down on his arms. He repeated it numerous times, putting all his life force into it. He didn't care about his life anymore. He had nothing to live for. All the people he had loved had died. *Maybe I'll be happier when I see them all.* A stream of energy ran through his chest and in his arms. His head swayed and the taste of blood formed in his mouth. Talmage saw Kadir's color returned to his face. The brown pigmentation on his forehead and cheeks grew brighter, but Talmage's vision began to blur. The stream of consciousness poured out into his arms, and down into his fingertips, his fingers melted into Kadir's chest.

"Vivens mortua," Talmage chanted as his head swayed and his vision darkened. A sudden gust of wind forced him off Kadir, breaking the bond of life between them, slamming his head into the ceiling, and sliding on the ground. Sweat dripped down his face and panted. He struggled to breathe and lift his head. Talmage lifted glanced at Kadir. In front of him, a figure stood in the passage. Its black flowing cape swayed in the soft breeze, and a hazy light glowed around it. Talmage squinted at the silhouette.

You are ready, Talmage. The figure spoke to his mind. *Nothing will be achieved if unmeasurable sacrifices aren't made, and today you were willing to prove yourself for this mooncalf. Greatness awaits you, Talmage.*

The figure lifted its arm and pointed to the passage beyond it.

"I can't leave him," Talmage replied, his throat stung as he spoke.

Don't waste your life on someone that hasn't treated you with what you deserve. Abandon him, Talmage. The figure was swallowed into the light, and Talmage held his hand up to block the glaring brightness. *I can't leave him.* He had never cared for his brother's companions, but at that moment, he felt an urge of righteousness to save him and rescue him from Pius' wicked games. It was the first time Talmage desired to stand up to his mentor and do what he believed was just.

Talmage crawled to Kadir's body and placed his hand under his nose. Soft puffs of air gently touched his skin. With a sigh of relief, Talmage slumped next to him. His lips cracked, and his head throbbed. Talmage stared at the radiant light, casting streaks of white up against the wet wall and revealing the scars across his torso. He grabbed Kadir's hand and clenched it, feeling the bones roll in his grip. Kadir returned a soft squeeze. Talmage smiled and let go of his hand.

Finally, his weariness ate the light, and he gave into his solemn eyes.

JAROMIR

Faint screams echoed in the distance. Jaromir awoke. Pains ran through his arm and his neck, and Morten dragged him back into the room, where it all started. A wave of hopelessness pressed on him. His chances of escape had vanished, and his weapon was gone.

"Ah. There's the one that snuck away. The one that abandoned his family." A soft wiry voice floated from the darkness.

Jaromir didn't have to ask who was speaking. The filthy sorcerer's voice was burned into his memory like a hot iron. *Was there another way out?* He thought as Pius lifted his arm with the broken wrist.

"I have eyes everywhere! I don't care that you killed Renold. I'm not surprised you were able to kill him with one hand. He was as useless as a bucket without a base. After killing him, did you really think you were going to escape with a broken wrist and using a rag?" He laughed. "You're awfully quiet, aren't you?" Pius said, turning and walking over to Zylah. "And so are you."

"Leave her alone," Jaromir demanded.

Zylah hung her head. Her body was covered in wax, and the candles above her head had almost finished simmering onto her.

"Ahh. You can talk." Pius spun around. "I missed what you

said. Could you repeat it, please?"

Jaromir repeated it.

Pius stroked his wispy black hair behind his ear. "My hearing is fading with my old age."

"Leave her alone," Jaromir said louder.

Pius leaned closer with one hand behind his ear and the other gesturing to him to repeat it. His hair was dangling over his face like long spider legs.

"Leave her alone!" Jaromir shouted. Pius leaned in, gesturing Jaromir to repeat his words. "LEAVE HER ALONE!" He bellowed at her, yet he continued to move closer.

"ARE YOU FUCKING DEAF? LEAVE HER—," Pius shoved the rag into his mouth, forcing it down his throat. Jaromir thrashed his body, trying to spit it out of his mouth with his tongue. Morten constricted his movements. He flailed his free arm at the sorcerer, Pius grabbed it and twisted, overpowering him. Jaromir spat the rag out, thrust his body out of Morten's grip, and bit down on Pius' hand, breaking the skin.

Pius shrieked. He released the rag and Jaromir's arm. Morten lunged to grab Jaromir, but he ducked and weaved towards the sorcerer. Pius conjured a long icy spear and stood next to Zylah. Jaromir stopped. The icy spear pressed into her neck. Jaromir saw the freezing tip melting with the heat of her skin.

Jaromir took shallow breaths.

"For the brief moment that you are alive, you will regret this." Pius held his arm up, showing the bite wound.

Jaromir tried to speak, but no words came from his mouth. Zylah lifted her head up. Her eyes glistened, and tears fell down her cheeks. Jaromir's throat tightened.

Pius' gaze filled with rage. A different side surfaced—a wickedness from the shadows deep within him. His nostrils flared as he forced the spear into her skin. Zylah shrieked and tossed her body. The chains and leather vest constricted her movements. Pius lodged the magick spear deeper into her neck.

"ZYLAH!" Jaromir screamed, jumping at Pius, but before he made it to him, Morten wrapped his thick arms around him. Holding him tight and forcing Jaromir to watch his wife suffer.

Pius twisted and turned the spear, crunching and ripping her neck muscles. Blood poured from the stab wound. Pius snapped it off and left the spearhead in her neck. A stream of water and blood weaved together, like braided hair, down her body.

Jaromir collapsed to his knees, hunched over, struggling to breathe. Tears fell down his cheek, and his heart dropped at the horrific sight before him.

Pius laughed. "Isn't it beautiful?" He bent down and forced Jaromir to stare at it.

"Zylah…" He whispered. A sweeping feeling of sorrow and remorse pressed down on him. *Why did I leave you?*

The glistening amber and solidified statue of his wife sparkled in the dim room. It was stained with her blood and tears. Pius stood and yanked a torch from the wall. The little flame cast a ghostly orange glow over Zylah.

"Betray me, and next time, it'll be you." Pius held the torch over Zylah.

Jaromir quivered and sank to the ground, sobbing and crying. Everything had been taken from him; all he had left was his brother, Talmage. Jaromir spat. *How am I going to get out of this?*

Pius paced around the room. He had evolved into a fear-hungry fiend, feeding off the scared and helpless. He tilted his head back and took a deep breath. Jaromir swore he saw the torches flicker as he drew in breaths.

"Why did she make me do that? Morten! Why?" Pius glided over like a shadow and kneeled next to Jaromir. "It wasn't my fault. You made me do this, Jaromir. Her death is your fault."

Jaromir clenched his fists and glared at the sorcerer. A warm radiance pressed against his leg as Morten squeezed him with his thick arms. *If it's not now, no one will stop him, and he'll bring more death and corruption to The Three Kingdoms. I must stop him.*

TALMAGE

Talmage woke. The light had faded, but a dull light reflected from the walls. Kadir stood over him. "Talmage, is that really you?"

Talmage flinched. "You scared the shit out of me." He scrambled onto his feet. "You know it's me."

"I'm so glad to see you." Kadir wrapped his hands around him and squeezed him.

"I've been with you the whole time. What's gotten into you?" It seemed as if Kadir hadn't been awake since they had been in the labyrinth together, as if he had lost his memory and wandered with him like a soulless ghoul.

Kadir scrunched his face in pain and stepped back.

"How's your back?" Talmage lifted Kadir's shirt to inspect the wound. It had stopped bleeding. A dark purple rim had formed around the edges, and the skin surrounding it was red. "It doesn't look too good, Kadir."

"It'll be okay," Kadir said, looking around at their predicament. "Where are we?"

Talmage smiled. "If you look around, we're in an underground tunnel."

"Yeah, no shit, but where is this tunnel?"

"I don't know, maybe we're somewhere near the inner walls of

Valenor." He considered at the dark passages stretching away from them. He had become accustomed to the darkness and the quietness. Talmage cleared his throat. "Do you remember how you got here?"

Kadir investigated his arms and legs. "Bits and pieces of it."

"Do you remember what happened to your back?"

"I remember…" He trailed off, touching the wet glimmering walls. "I was leaving Valenor with Shaydin. We waited for Jaromir, he was meant to meet us, but he never showed up. Instead, we were attacked by sorcerers. They beat the shit out of me. I don't know what happened to Shaydin. Whether he got away or not, I don't know."

"Did Pius attack you?"

"I'd remember his ugly face. Did Jaromir end up finding you?" Kadir asked.

"What do you mean?" Talmage seemed confused. His brother hadn't cared for him at all, especially in the last few years.

"Shaydin and I went to his house before we left, and there was a note. It said he went looking for you, along with other orders."

"Jaromir doesn't care about me. Why would he look for me?"

"That's a lie, and you know it," Kadir said, stumbling towards him.

"It's not. I know the truth. I know the truth about him and the order." Talmage shut his fists and squeezed them with his burning anger. "Jaromir killed Agustin. The only person in this world that took us in when no one would."

Kadir hung his head. "I know. I was there."

Talmage grabbed Kadir by the scruff of his shirt, taking deep breaths. "You were there?"

"He was a sorcerer!" Kadir shoved his hands off and stepped back.

"I should've let you die!" At that moment, Talmage wanted to conjure magick, make Kadir suffer for what he had done. "I shouldn't have listened to Pius. I should've let you rot in this place."

"Did Pius tell you to kill me? Is he in here with us?" Kadir hobbled towards him, wincing at the pain in his back.

"No, he isn't. I thought you might've been different, but you're not! You're the same as the rest!"

"That's why we all joined the order. We all want to rid the

world of magick. Never let it rise through the ranks of society."

"You'll have to kill me then." Talmage smirked at him. At last, he had said the words to someone other than his mentors. The words soothed his aching secrecy and struggling for his own liberation.

Kadir lunged at Talmage, slammed him against the cold wall. He forced his forearm into Talmage's neck, choking him. "Jaromir knew there was something strange about you. He probably didn't want to think it or believe it could've been possible."

Talmage struggled under his force. For an injured man, Kadir had great strength over Talmage.

"The funny thing is Tal. There was a moment I pitied you. I stuck my neck out for you, and I tried to include you with your brother's plans. What you're doing is going against everything he believes in and what the order is fighting against." He pressed his arm against his neck, "How could you be so stupid?"

Talmage clawed his fingers around his arm and shoved Kadir off. He took gasps of air. "Have you ever tried to live in the shadow of greatness? My whole life has been shadowed by Jaromir's success. His swordsmanship and confidence. What else was I meant to do? Agustin and Pius filled the void that was missing in my soul."

Kadir stumbled, pressing his hand on his back. He leaned on the wall in agony. "You could've spoken to someone about it. You could've done anything else than scurry under the wings of a wicked sorcerer. Anything!" Kadir bellowed.

"You don't understand, and you never will," Talmage muttered.

"You're a fucking coward. If I die down here, you deserve to perish in these tunnels with me." Kadir launched at Talmage. The pair tumbled down the passage, gripping and shoving one another. Kadir tried to contain him, but Talmage wriggled free from his grip and pulled himself up. He wanted to beat the life out of him, but he remembered something Pius had once warned him about. *Be careful of the wounded man.*

"You betrayed your family and your kingdom." Kadir crouched and took a deep breath "How do you think Jaromir will react when he hears this?"

"He won't care! He never has and he never will!" Sweat dripped down Talmage's face and his heart thudded in his throat.

"Deep down, do you really think your brother doesn't care

about you?"

Talmage studied the injured man. His face grew pale, and lips were pale. "All he cares about is the order. I know he'll kill me when he finds out who I really am, just like he did with Agustin."

"Stop spewing shit from your mouth. Jaromir was looking for you."

Talmage frowned, panting. "How do I know you're not lying?"

"What else do I have to lose? Jaromir wanted to repair the broken bond. I know he did."

All the anger that had stirred in him for his brother resided. "He killed Agustin. I can't forgive him for that."

"He doesn't seek your forgiveness. It was what he had been trained to do. You know that more than anyone."

Talmage hung his head forward and sighed. *He's right. He's speaking the truth, but my heart cannot forgive Jaromir. Not yet.* A hand fell on Talmage's shoulder, breaking his thoughts.

"I'm sorry I lashed out at you. I still hate you for using magick." Kadir smirked.

Talmage nodded and gripped his hand.

"I swear on my life, what I said, it's the truth. Jaromir cares about you, even if you have followed a different path. The bond of brothers is stronger than any forged metal in the world. Bound together by blood. Nothing will ever break it."

For a moment, Kadir comforted Talmage. He coughed into his shoulder. "Dying in here is what scares me the most, Kadir."

Kadir looked at the dark passage. "Before, why did you say Pius told you to kill me?"

"Pius wanted me to kill you and save myself."

"Is he in here? Did you follow him?"

"It spoke to me in my mind." Talmage stood up and looked at the way they had come from. A memory flashed of him struggling with Morten and Renold. Talmage had thrown his fists and kicked them as they'd restrained him and dragged him away.

"Thank you." Kadir patted him on the shoulder, pulling him back to the dark underground tunnels, and turned him around. "Thank you for keeping me alive, for a little bit longer. I hope Asa isn't a part of this."

Talmage's gaze lowered, thinking of the memory.

"Are you okay?" Kadir shook Talmage's shoulder.

"Yeah, I was just thinking of when I was brought down here."

"If you were so chumming with the *innocent sorcerer*, why would he drag you down here? That doesn't make sense."

"It's all a test." Talmage looked at Kadir. His narrow face frowned at him. "Pius wanted me to be the next monarch. I wanted to be it, but…" The trials of his ghosts lingered. He had been training for several years, and he had desired to rule over the people and his brother. "I don't know what I want anymore," Talmage mumbled.

"I know I'm not getting out of here, but you are, Talmage. When you do, learn from your mistakes. Don't live a life in the shadows. Embrace the light as if it was Agustin."

Talmage's heart tightened. "How do I know that's the right thing to do?"

"I'm not asking you. I'm fucking ordering you. You got that?" Kadir grabbed his shirt and pulled him closer. His breath reeked of rotten eggs, and the awful pungent stench of his wound stung his nostrils.

Talmage nodded. *Maybe he's right.*

Kadir let go of him. "Good. Now let's get you out of here." He limped towards the light, pressing his hand against his back like an elderly man with a hunch.

"You're too weak." Talmage ran his hand through his hair and observed the fading light. It radiated in the distance but softer than before.

Kadir ignored him and continued, struggling to stand on his own feet and limping in the soft milky light. A familiarity bestowed on Talmage as he walked alongside Kadir. The injured man grunted and staggered as if they were leaving the Amalgamate tavern after a long, heavy night on the ale. Talmage welcomed the conjured fantasy like an old acquaintance, smiling at the acceptance of his past and desires to someone other than a ghost.

"What do you think that light could be?" Kadir asked, holding onto Talmage.

The two lost men stumbled towards the blurred light in the distance.

"I hope it's outside," Talmage answered, shifting his shoulders under Kadir's armpit, "but I think you should rest."

"Not yet… We're almost there." Kadir's lips stuck together with each word.

Talmage offered him his damp shirt and some moss, but he

moved his head away from it. "You need to eat it and rest," he ordered him.

Kadir slipped out of Talmage's grasp and stumbled over. Pressing against the wall, he slid down to the ground. "Not the food... Maybe... we rest for a bit."

Talmage slumped down next to him against the cold wall. His shoulders and lower back ached from dragging the wounded messenger. Kadir rested on the rock wall with his eyes closed. His face had lost more color, and his lips were streaked blue with purple veins.

"It could be morning." Kadir's voice was faint, like a breeze drifting from the white glow.

They seemed so close, but they had ventured towards it for hours. It never loomed within reach, always dangling in front of them, teasing and taunting them. He could taste the smoky rays of fog from a fire on a winter's morning. Agustin had always made sure there was always fire on the cold mornings. Jaromir and Talmage had once enjoyed each other's company before Talmage had caught Agustin starting the campfire with his magick. The thought brought a tear to his eye.

"Or it could be a fire." Kadir interrupted Talmage's thoughts.

"Wouldn't there be smoke?"

"Not if it was ventilated like a furnace." Kadir shifted his backside, wincing and moaning at each movement. His back had stopped bleeding, but it was heavily infected. Talmage flinched at the stench of spoiled meat seeping out of Kadir's clothing with each wriggle.

"I wonder if Pius made these passages just for our torture," Kadir said, shifting his backside. "That would've taken him years."

"Not with his magick. He has the power beyond anything I've ever seen before." Talmage answered, rubbing his hands together. The icy breeze sent a chill up his arms.

Kadir coughed and shrieked from the pain from his back. Talmage looked at him. Kadir's chest rose and fell in shallow breaths.

"We need to keep moving." Kadir struggled to pull himself up. Talmage quickly grabbed under his arm and helped him up.

Kadir forced himself to stand, grunting and scrunching his face with each movement of his back. Talmage gripped his shoulders, and they began walking towards the radiating light. Talmage spat, feeling his throat tense and eyes dry up with the soft breeze coming from up ahead. He pulled his tunic collar to soothe his parched mouth. The water provided little relief, but it was all they had to survive. He didn't want to journey back to the lake. It would consume too much time and, by then, it might be too late for Kadir.

He's nearly gone. He thought, staring at the ghostly face of the wounded man. Kadir's weight pressed down on his shoulders as they limped together in the passage. Talmage had patted down the injured man's face, but all that had done was wipe the sweat off his fading face. *If only I could use magick.* Talmage glanced at the dried blood on the back of Kadir's shirt. The bleeding had ceased, but the part of the shirt that stuck to the wound was a black circle, and it began to reek of spoiled meat.

"You never told me how you got that gash on your back," Talmage said, looking at this companion.

Kadir moaned. "I… I don't know…" His voice was soft and croaky. "Maybe you did it." He smiled.

Talmage laughed. "You seriously don't remember how you got it?"

"Um… it was two big men. I tried to fight them. I… I think…,"

They ambled along the passageway towards the mysterious light, which Talmage assumed, was the end of his trial. He squinted and held his hand up to cover his face from the glare.

"We're nearly there, Kadir, and then we can get you some help." Talmage felt Kadir's body fall forward. He looked at him, and his eyes were closed. He shook the limp body. "See, look ahead. We're almost there. Stay with me, Kadir."

"I told you… you're making it…"

"I told you that we are both making it out of here, alive." Talmage tilted his head to check on him. The wrinkles on Kadir's face had relaxed, and his mouth was slightly open.

"Stay with me!" Talmage sat him down and rested him against the wall. "Kadir. Kadir! Wake up!" He tapped his cheeks. "Wake up. Come on, Kadir, please." Talmage's eyes swelled up, and his throat tightened.

Talmage pressed his fingers against Kadir's neck. Talmage began to panic, and his hands trembled as he placed it under his nose. "Come on, Kadir." He grabbed his face and slapped them softly. Kadir was not responding. Talmage hit harder and harder until a rage poured over him. He knocked Kadir across the face.

"Wake up!" Talmage bellowed at him. His mouth trembled, and tears covered his vision.

"Vivens mortua," he chanted, willing to sacrifice his own life, but it proved useless. He gave up and fell to next to him. Talmage wanted to curl in a ball and wake up, to hope all of it was a nightmare; his whole life was a nightmare. Everything he had done was for nothing. All the trials and training to be a ruler were a waste of time. He didn't want to be the person people relied on. He wanted to wake up in Tarnsby with his parents and brother—before he had burned everything and before Jaromir had murdered Agustin. The heartache of his brother's betrayal haunted his mind. *Why would he do it?*

For a while, Talmage lay with his thoughts, contemplating his life. He fell in and out of sleep, holding onto Kadir's lifeless body. He stared at the illuminating light. *I can't give up.* Clenching his hand, a flame of hope ignited in his arms like a phoenix resurrecting from the ashes.

Talmage forced himself up and wiped away his tears. "Stay here." He told the lifeless body. "I'm going to get help." He stumbled towards the bright light, pushing through the pains and aches of his overtired body. *Once this is over, I'm returning home with or without Jaromir. He can live with the guilt of his life, but I can't do it anymore. I'm done with people and their wicked ways.*

Talmage staggered through the harsh white light like a curtain dangling in over the passage. He squinted and held his hands up, covering his vision. Slowly, he walked into the whiteness, narrowing his eyes.

Thud.

Talmage fell, slamming his head on the ground, and his sight turned to black.

JAROMIR

Pius grunted and flattened the creases in his robe. "I should've killed you before all of this got out of hand. I should've re-opened that scar on your arm, but I admire the vigor you possess. Before you suffer just as Zylah did, there is one thing you should know."

Jaromir peered at him, watching his every move. The sorcerer's robe swayed behind him, revealing a dagger on his waist. "What should I know?" he asked, feeling his palms sweat.

Pius snickered. "Emperors haven't been the greatest rulers of the Three Kingdoms. I despise them, and I will dispose of all that oppose me—including that Empress Suiko, she's next on my list, after you." He smiled at Jaromir. His thin wicked yellow teeth reflected the torchlight. "I serve the kingdoms and what it once was; full of magick. You killed one of my very loyal servants, but now, the blood must run thick on my hands." He turned and strolled to the wall of tools and grabbed the long scissors off it. He twisted and observed the instrument as he wandered back over to Jaromir. Pius crouched before him. "Any last words?" He smiled.

Jaromir stole a look at Morten as he tightened his grip around his arms. The servant watched his master glare at Jaromir. The rusty hinges squeaked as Pius squeezed them, and the sharp blades reflected the torchlight.

Jaromir's attention was brought back to the vile sorcerer. "At one point, I wanted to tell you where I sent my messengers, but I'm glad I didn't. Do you think you will get out of this alive, Pius? I now know that you were training Talmage, but that doesn't change how I feel about magick. You speak of wealth and greatness with justice, but I won't let you destroy this world. I WON'T!" Jaromir refused to give in to the sorcerer. His heart raced beneath his shirt, and he wished he had the sickle to end it once and for all.

Pius' nostrils flared, and his wet black hair shone in the torchlight. "You see, primitive fool. I wanted the truth from you and Talmage. I wanted Talmage to be the next monarch ruler for my bidding, but he showed me blatant signs of his weakness along the way. I threw him in the underground tunnels below with your comrade Kadir to test that weakness of his. My men have dealt with all your doings to refute your order. Your home is gone. Your comrades, and now your wife, are all dead, and you will join them, soon enough." Pius stood and spread his arms. "You were a pawn in this upheaval, and I simply needed the time to remove all your allies. All of this was all a fun game for me—a pastime if you say."

A fun game. Jaromir fixed his glare at the ground. *A pastime.* "You murdered Zylah and my comrades!" He shouted and closed his usable hand as he held it behind his back. Shivers ran down Jaromir's spine and into his stomach as he took deep breaths.

"You are the one to blame for their deaths. Not me." Pius stared deeply at Zylah's sculptured face. "I didn't want to hurt you." His voice softened, and he turned around, with narrow dark eyes. "It was your fault I did this. YOUR FAULT!" He spun and punched Zylah's head, snapping it off and shattering to pieces on the floor.

Jaromir's heart dropped. His arms tingled as he clenched his hand in growing fury. He breathed deeply as he focused on his task. *His last task.*

Morten held him back with his strength. Jaromir hung his head, closed his eyes, and let his body go limp. The brute stumbled forward, holding Jaromir's body weight.

"What is it?" Pius paced over, his boots tapping on the stone floor. He lifted Jaromir's chin.

Jaromir slightly opened one of his eyes and saw a blurry vision of Pius standing before him. A dim gleam reflected off his waist.

"What do you think you're doing, fool?" Pius asked, observing his face with the scissors. "Playing dead is fit for a rat. Suppose it does suit your character." Pius lowered the tool from his face.

Jaromir opened his eyes and lunged himself at Pius, tackling him to the ground. The pair rolled along the ground, both the scissors and dagger sliding away from them. Crunching and slamming their limbs on the shattered wax and hard floor.

"You fool!" Pius fumbled with Jaromir's arms.

A sharp pain ran through Jaromir's wrist, but he focused on his task. His last attempt to escape alive. He tumbled on top of the sorcerer, pinning down his arms. Pius recited magick words, launched spells at him, but Jaromir aimed his hands toward the ceiling. Magick bounced off the walls and rattled the chains that held Zylah's headless body.

Frustration crinkled Pius' face, and his grotesque teeth snarled at him. "Save me, Morten!"

"Don't help him." Jaromir forced his knee into the sorcerer's thigh. The sorcerer winced and flailed his body.

Morten hesitated.

"You don't have to help him. He's not going to hurt you anymore." Jaromir pleaded.

"Don't listen to him!" Pius thrashed his body.

Jaromir struggled to hold him down. "He's going to kill us all, Morten. Don't you see that?"

Pius jerked his hips, tossing Jaromir across the floor, wax stabbing into his skin. Jaromir smacked his head on the table. His head swayed as he scrambled up but he fell onto the ground. The dagger slid across the floor towards Morten.

The sorcerer jumped up and stood above Jaromir. "You have no idea what you've unleashed within me." Pius conjured an icy spear, his eyes reflecting the mystifying blue. He held it over his head.

"Throw it here! Before it's too late!" Jaromir shouted to Morten.

The sorcerer spun around. Morten slid the dagger across the ground towards Jaromir, but his aim was off. It bounced off the wall behind him.

Pius hysterical laugh filled the room. Jaromir crawled towards the dagger.

"You're too late, rodent. No one is coming to save you."

As Pius finished his words, a faint scream came from the corner of the room. From the enclosed well. All of a sudden, a blow stole his vision and replaced it with a void of darkness.

Tal...

TALMAGE

A piercing shot of pain ran through Talmage's head as he opened his eyes. He squinted against the white light glaring around him. The icy wind sent goose pimples all over his body. The walls surrounding him were a brilliant white with torches enclosed in ivory glass cases. The flames did not flicker or make a shadow. Talmage stood up, rubbing his head, and scrutinized the strangeness. He caressed the surface and put his ear up against it. A slight humming noise came from it, and a cold wind poured onto his ankles. Glancing at the base, he noticed an inch-long thin gap stretching along it. He crouched down and placed his hand inside the crack. Talmage embraced the breath of winter on his rough fingertips and singed palms and stuck his head in the small opening.

"Help!" He shouted into it. "Is anyone there? Kadir needs urgent help!" Talmage waited and listened. The deep, howling sounds of the wind flowed around his face. He pounded his fists on the smooth surface. It seemed different from the labyrinth. *Is this mortar?* He glanced around as his heart beat faster.

He shouted for help but no response.

Searching around the blocked exit, Talmage scanned over the surface for any imperfections. He searched the ground for loose rocks or stones, but it was clean. To die in the blank and untouched space seemed too contrasting to his miserable life. He squinted at the roof. Its radiating white walls stretched high into a narrow hole like a well.

Talmage knew it was the end of the labyrinth, but instead of being relieved and overjoyed that he had escaped the catacombs of the underground passages, he was left with confusion and doubt. It was not the end he was expecting. He could not comprehend what was happening above, but he didn't want to stay there any longer. *I need to climb up it.* He concluded. An eerie feeling descended him. He glanced upward at the light, then ran back into the darkness. "Kadir, where are you?" His eyes had adjusted to the whiteness, but as he roamed into the shadows, putting his hands out in front of him, he felt blind. He stumbled on something and fell to the cold hard ground. He scrambled to his knees, feeling a soft damp object. He peered at his surroundings. A faint silhouette came apparent before him.

Talmage climbed over Kadir's body to his jaw and tapped it. "Kadir! Are you there? Come on..." Talmage's hands trembled with each tap on his cold cheeks.

Kadir's head bobbed with each tap, but his face didn't respond. Talmage placed his hand under his nose.

"Wake up. Please! We're almost out of this shit hole! You can't leave me!" Talmage continued to shake, trying to wake him. "You coward, you can't give up..." Tears fell from his eyes as he tried to revive his companion.

Sniffing his nose and wiping the tears from his cheeks, Talmage continued to shake him. His vision had adjusted to the darkness, and he could see his face. It was pale white, and his eyes were rolled into the back of his head.

Talmage sighed. He caressed his cheek and closed his eyes. *I'll come back for you. I promise.*

He stood and left him behind. Leaving the shadows of the labyrinth behind, he welcomed the white walls with a renewed sense of hope and determination. He looked upward. The narrow hole rose higher from the torches. He glanced around to see if anything could help him up, nothing but rocks and darkness. The roof of the passage rose sharply to the narrow hole. He did a quick test and jumped up, scratching the ceiling with his fingertips. The gap was two to three feet above his head, but he had no way of pulling himself up. He glanced around. Sweat formed in his singed palms. The end seemed near yet high above and out of reach.

Talmage looked at the torches. The glass globes enclosed the flame and morphed it to a bright light that stood motionless within it like a soul in a human's body. An urge of strength stirred within him. He ripped the globe off the fixture and threw it down, shattering the glass. He seized the torch from its metal case and tossed it into the darkness.

In the dim light, Talmage craned his neck and judged how high the narrow hole was from the torch fixture. At shoulder height, Talmage gripped onto the warm metal case and hung from it. Relieved with the outcome, Talmage's plan was to leap high enough from the torch holder and up the narrow hole. It was risky, but it was the only choice he had. He mused at the white fixture. A memory of Agustin came to his mind. He had been with his brother and guardian, sitting around a campfire after a group of bandits had mugged them. Agustin was mending a wound on Talmage's arm. Agustin had saved their lives, but they had lost everything.

"Weren't you scared?" Talmage had asked Agustin.

"Fear isn't something we should avoid, Tal." Agustin wrapped a bit of torn shirt around his arm. "Without fear, how could someone be courageous?"

Jaromir stood up. "What do you mean? Those bandits almost killed us! They were probably sorcerers trying to finish the job."

Agustin looked at him, his eyes reflecting the small campfire. "When I was younger, I learned that courage could not exist without fear like hate and love. My father told me, "a brave man is not someone that doesn't feel fear or afraid but instead conquers and triumphs over that fear." Agustin had looked at Talmage and smiled. A smile Talmage would never forget.

Talmage absently gazed at the passage, reflecting on that night. He paced to the opposite side of the wall. He closed his eyes and took a few deep breaths. Running towards the wall, feeling the cold breeze gush past his legs, he leaped for the torch holder, his grip slipped, and he landed on the hard ground, crushing his shoulder.

He howled and pounded the ground with his fist. Talmage stood up, brushed the dust off his shirt, and went to the opposite side of the wall. He took a breath and leaped for the torch holder, grabbing it, and swinging himself up, but his foot missed the ledge. His body weight and momentum swung him off, slamming him back onto the ground. "Fuck!" he bellowed. A burning pain shooting through his arm, but he stood up and rolled his arms around, shaking it off.

Come on. A third time, he paced to the other side and leaped at the torch holder. His right-foot landed in the fixture. He pulled himself up and balanced. Taking shallow breaths, he studied how far he had to jump to the upward opening.

He readied his next leap, bouncing for momentum. *One...* Talmage gauged where he needed to jump. *Two...* His idea to leap and press his hands up against each side like a star and hope with the momentum, he could hold himself up. Talmage wasn't sure if it was going to work, but he had no other choice.

He swung his arms.

"Three!" He shouted as he leaped up the hole. Rocks crumbled under his palms as he forced his arms on the walls of the opening. He tensed his shoulders and dug his heels into the wall, but he slipped. As his hands dragged down the wall, he felt a gap—an inward-facing step at the bottom of the narrow upward hole—before crashing on the ground.

The impact thud through his lungs. He grasped his ribs and held his breath. Talmage tried to take breaths, but his airway was tight. He wanted to yell out in pain. He took short and shallow breaths.

After a while, his muscles relaxed, and he could breathe properly. He stood, stretched his shoulders, and stepped back, searching for the ledge. He jumped on the torch and leapt for the step. His palms grazed the wall, but he couldn't grip. He landed on his feet.

"Fuck!" He screamed in frustration. *Why can't I grab it?* He glanced at his sweaty and singed palms. He rubbed them on his shirt, trying to remove the moisture, he jumped onto the torch. His thighs and calves burned from exhaustion. As he stood on the torch handle, he wiped his hands for safe measure. Without counting down, he leaped up the hole and gripped the edge with his right hand. He held himself up long enough to grasp it with his other hand. Panting hard and dangling in the hole. He looked around for another step, nothing but a flat surface. He pulled his legs up and pressed them against the narrow sides, fixing them flat as he stretched out his right-hand to the other side. He pushed his right-hand up the passage until his torso was high enough to place his feet into the step. Standing on the narrow hole with his arms pressing on the side, he felt like he was leaning over the edge of a cliff, dangling over the difference between life and death. The sweat ran down his jaw, tickling his skin.

Talmage searched for more steps while resting for a moment and taking deep breaths. He glanced and peered into the narrow wall space, but there were no other indent or spaces to scale higher. Small cracks stretched up the wall, with thin vines running up the wall. *They're too thin and weak to mount.*

In the forest outside Tarnsby, he used to climb up trees in the forest to watch the world flow beneath him as if he were a bird, where no one would take notice of him.

His feet shifted in the small gap, bringing his attention to the awkward angle of his back, stretched across the opening. As he pressed his hand on the side

I've got to keep going. Talmage placed his right foot on the opposite wall, putting some of his body weight on it to fix it into a slight crack in the wall. He shifted his hand on the cold rock wall and sprung his body into the center of the passage. Spread between the narrow opening, he hung like a star in the night sky.

Talmage slowly balanced his weight from his right leg to left hand and climbed with opposite sides like a spider crawling up its web towards its prey. Creeping upwards towards the way out, he hoped. Talmage's arms and legs burned from exhaustion and sweat dripped down his back. He placed his legs and hands in the walls' cracks to help support his feet and palms. The cold wind howled past him, and muffled voices came from above.

He stopped.

His deep breaths filled the tight space, and his heart raced. He looked up and stopped for the voices again.

"Hello?" He shouted. "Help me!" He waited for a short while, but his shoulders and arms began to shake, and his ankles trembled. *I've got to keep going.* He continued climbing, suppressing his aching limbs.

As he made his way further up, the end creeping closing and pushing through his burning arms and legs, vines intertwining with the cracks. A muffled shout echoed from above. Talmage ignored it and climbed higher. The narrow sides thinned as he scaled up the passage.

An unmistakable voice shouted. "Before it's too late."

"Help!" He screamed out. His hands were slipping, and the rocks under his feet began to crumble.

A loud ting rang from above.

Talmage tried to rush higher towards the roof, shifting his weight from opposite limbs to ascend the wall. Dodging the thin vines, he crept up. More piercing noises and grunting voices grew louder. A whooshing sweep echoed from above. An exhilarating surge of survival and freedom ran through him as he reached the top. His head rammed against a closed opening. He fixed his legs into the uneven surface and banged against the blockade.

"Is someone there?" Panic raced through Talmage's body as he pounded on the obstacle. His body was crammed up against it, and his legs trembled, slowly crumbling in the crack.

"Don't open it!" A voice shouted from the other side.

With one final push, he shoved upward and flipped the lid off to the side. A stench of horse manure and an acidic bile taste stung Talmage's nostrils. His throat tensed up, and he held his breath as he pulled himself up and over the edge.

What he witnessed was not what he expected.

"You're earlier than I anticipated." Pius stood up from Jaromir's body.

Talmage's neck tensed at the scene before him. There was too much for him to take in, but one thing was certain—Jaromir was on the ground, unconscious and missing a hand.

"What are you doing?" Talmage muttered. He thought he would have been pleased to see that his brother had suffered for his ways of life but a strange sense of unjust stirred within him.

"Are you that blind and ignorant?"

Jaromir... Talmage frowned at him. "Why?"

"He killed my friend! He killed our people! Don't you see how poisonous Jaromir is to this new world we're trying to create? We can't let him infect it." Pius snarled. He paced over, grabbed the dagger off the ground, and put it back on his waist.

Talmage saw a different side to him. An irrational and unpredictable side to him, which he did not trust. "You can't do this. He's my brother." He rushed over and stood between Jaromir and Pius.

"Don't just stand there, Morten, dispose of him."

Morten hesitated.

Pius spun around. "Didn't you hear me? Grab him!" He

bellowed. Morten stepped back with widened eyes and shook his head.

"Now is the time you choose to disobey me? Very well."

Before Talmage could blink, an icy spear pierced through Morten's neck. Pinning the large man up the wall. Blood poured over the white magick weapon, and Talmage stared at it with horror. Morten had been Pius' loyal servant for as long as he could remember. For Pius to rid of him so easily, it confirmed his distrust in the wicked sorcerer. *There's no ward here.* He realized, clenching his fist.

A hand grabbed Talmage's ankle. He glanced at it. Jaromir looked up at him with blood covering his face. "Run," he mouthed.

"You've awoken," Pius said, with a shrill voice, leaving the brute pinned against the wall.

Talmage's mouth narrowed and he squeezed his hand. His mentor's black hair glistened in the candlelight. "How could you do that to Morten?"

"Don't worry, we can always get another servant. I'm sure there are more than enough people willing to serve you once you become the next ruler."

"Do you think I want to reign with you?" Talmage shouted at him.

"You ungrateful little brat. You have no idea what I went through to get you where you are today! I can take it all away from you as fast as I took that halfwit down!" Pius launched an icy spear at him.

"Ardeat ignis." Talmage warded it off with his fire spell. He felt his chest tightened. The flames melted the spear to a puddle in the middle of the small dark room.

Talmage smirked at him.

"Get out of here, Jar."

"Distract him," Jaromir told him, crawling to the wall.

Talmage looked down at his brother. His face was smeared with exhaustion and blood. He had despised him for killing the only person that took him in, but as Talmage stared at Jaromir, he could see he had suffered for all his wrongs.

"This day has come sooner than I expected." Pius' thin husky voice carried across the darkroom.

"I've had enough of the killing. I've had enough of your just ways! You had no right to kill Morten. No right!" Talmage lifted his gaze.

"He was my servant. I had the only right!"

"You preached justice and tradition, but you've undone everything you go by. I don't want to be the next ruler, and you won't have that chance." Talmage was breathing deep and clenching his fists. "If I must take you down to save the innocent lives, so be it. One of us is walking out of here, Pius, and it isn't you."

Pius' black eyes beaming at him like a snake ready to strike. Behind him, he heard Jaromir rummage along the walls. Pius' eyes were locked on Talmage.

"You can never defeat me, Talmage! You're too weak!" Pius launched an icy spear towards Talmage.

He deflected the blow with another spell. His chest tightened at the cost of his spells but he concealed his fatigue. "You've grown old and slow."

Pius charged at him with a battle cry, summoning an electrifying spell in his hand. Talmage lunged to intercept his attack, tackling him. Pius cast the spell, missing him, and bouncing off the walls. Talmage gripped Pius' wrists and pinned him on the floor. "With your age, you've lost your strength."

"Don't get too cocky, boy!" Pius propelled his hips upward and threw him off.

He tumbled across the ground. Pius bounded over and pinned him down. His knees pressed into Talmage's upper arms and he cast an icy block over his legs. Talmage tried to kick the ice frozen over his legs. He tossed and flailed, but Pius was too heavy. His legs were pinned and Pius rolled his knees around on his arms.

Talmage howled in pain. "Jaromir!" He yelled for help.

Before Pius could lift his head from Talmage's eyes, Jaromir tackled him.

"Now's your chance, Talmage! Grab the dagger off him!"

Pius grunted and struggled with Jaromir. "GET OFF ME!"

Jaromir tightened his grip around the sorcerer. "Now, Talmage!"

Talmage cast a flame and melted the ice on his legs. He stood up, ducking, and weaving the spells bouncing off and fading into the darkness. He paced over. Pius stopped squirming like a fish out of water and glared at Talmage.

"This is your only chance. It's now or never!" Jaromir begged.

"Can you really trust him, Talmage? He killed Agustin." Pius pleaded, trying to wriggle from his hold, shooting magick from his hands all around the room. "He knows you wield magick. He'll betray you and murder you when you least expect it."

Jaromir's eyes widened at him. "Don't believe him! He'll say anything to stay alive. Look how easily he killed Morten."

"Was it easy to kill Agustin?" Talmage glared at Jaromir.

"Don't fall into his traps. Look what he's doing to us!"

"Answer the question, *brother*."

Jaromir tightened his grip around the sorcerer's limbs. "No, it wasn't easy. I did what I was trained to do, just like you can do right know."

Talmage pondered on the predicament. "I could leave both of you to die in here and all my problems would disappear." Talmage stared at his brother, smiling, and tucking a long strand of hair behind his ear. On Pius' waist, the dagger reflected the dim candlelight. Sweat dripped down Talmage's face, tickling his neck. "I could close and lock the door. Walk away, without any repercussions. You two would remain and eventually kill one another."

Pius' black eyes gleamed at him. He smirked underneath his oily dark hair. "Leave your treacherous brother, not me. I saved you, Talmage. I showed you the true path of salvation."

"You wouldn't dare leave us in here," Jaromir said.

"Don't tempt me." Talmage reached for the dagger.

Pius squirmed. Jaromir tensed his arms and legs, wincing his face and constricting Pius' movements, aiming his hands away from Talmage.

Talmage seized the dagger and studied it in the light. "You're right, brother. I don't have it in me to leave you in here but you, Pius, on the other hand."

"You filthy maggots. The both of you. You both deserve to perish." Pius' words were stolen by a gasp of air. His mouth slowly filled with blood.

Talmage stabbed the dagger into Pius' chest. Twisting into his skin and crunching the bones as the blade dug deeper, blood squirting onto him and on the floor. Jaromir shifted from behind him and let his body drop. The sorcerer's legs buckled, and he clawed at his killer. Talmage craned his neck away, pushing the blade deeper into his chest. Blood splattering and covering his face.

"That's enough, Talmage." Jaromir pulled him away.

Talmage took deep breaths, his hands trembling. He stared at his mentor drifting into the underworld.

"You had me worried, Tal. It's good to see you." Jaromir patted him on the back with his uninjured hand.

"I'm sorry but it was the only way to have him hanging on my words. It's good to see you, too."

The brothers wrapped their arms around each other.

A wave of sadness overcame Talmage. For years, his past had haunted him, his brother had neglected him and murdered Agustin, but as he hugged into Jaromir's warm chest, a heavy burden lifted from his soul. The twins welcomed each others presence for a moment in the dark room.

The candles softly flickered, and the chains made soft rattling noises. Dripping blood tapped on the ground from Morten's body on the wall and the shuffling noises from Pius' limbs shifted on the ground.

"It's not over yet." Jaromir broke the intimate moment, pulling from him. "We need to get out of here."

Talmage gazed around the room. Blood and yellow pieces of crystal were scattered across the ground, with disfigured dead bodies on the floor. His heart dropped, and his breath was ripped from his lungs at the sight of death. In the far dark corner, opposite to the one exit, he saw a headless statue. Its surface glowed in an off-yellow substance.

"What happened here?" Talmage asked, staring at Jaromir.

Jaromir's neck was stained with the same yellow substance and wine. "I'll tell you when we get out of here."

As Jaromir limped towards the stone door, he stopped and knelt over at the statue. He kissed the solidified hand. Talmage turned and approached Pius. His hand trembled as he crouched over and removed the dagger. Twisting and crunching the blade, blood splashed and oozed from the wound. His mentor's eyes absently gazed at the wall, with his mouth gaped open.

The brave man conquered and triumphed over the fear. Talmage didn't feel sad about the loss of his mentor. A heavy weight had been lifted, and the ghosts of his past had rested in peace. He could live a life without magick. He could go home and live his days in peace.

The stone door swung open, shining a faint light onto the room. A man stood in the doorway.

Jaromir climbed to his feet. Talmage held the dagger out in front of him.

Jaromir stepped towards. figure. "Shaydin? Is that you?"

"It stinks in here." Shaydin glanced around at the darkroom.

"How did you know we were here?" Jaromir asked, approaching him, and wrapping his arms around him.

Talmage sneered at his brother squeezing the soldier draped in a long leather cloak.

"Zylah told me." Shaydin pulled from him and glanced at Talmage. Shaydin's eyes peered at Talmage holding the weapon, and the blood scattered over his body.

"I'm glad to see you." Jaromir intercepted Shaydin's gaze. "I see you didn't make it to our meeting point. Where's Kadir?"

Talmage lowered the weapon, cautious of his brother's comrade. He did not want to have any more secrets. "Kadir didn't make it. He's down there." He pointed to the well.

"Was this your doing?" Shaydin approached him, reaching for his sword on his waist.

"I did everything to save him!"

"Not everything." Shaydin unsheathed his sword and held it at Talmage's throat. The cold blade pressed on his neck.

"Enough!" Jaromir bellowed. "Withdraw from him, Shaydin."

For a moment, Shaydin studied Talmage. Talmage held the dagger out, his hands shaking. Shaydin sheathed his sword and returned to Jaromir's side.

"I'll explain everything to you on the way out." Jaromir nodded at Talmage.

Shaydin began walking and Jaromir held out his closed hand to Talmage.

He hesitantly walked towards his brother.

"I've got something for you." Jaromir opened his hand, and the necklace dropped. Talmage caught it and held it out in front of him. It was the necklace Talmage had received from Agustin. Its cloudy stone within the necklace reflected the light shining in the doorway. Even though Jaromir had killed Agustin, he sensed he had forgiven him for using magick behind his back.

"The bond of brothers is stronger than any forged metal in the world. Bound together by blood, and nothing can break it." Talmage's chest tensed, and tears ran down his cheeks.

Jaromir pulled him closer. "That's something Kadir used to tell me."

The three exited the dark lifeless room. Talmage was free of responsibilities, free of his ghosts, and free to live how he should have from the beginning. A life that was not dictated by his past and from his own choices. A life that his parents wouldn't be ashamed of. *We were proud of you no matter what, Talmage and Jaromir...* A whisper lingered in the tunnel. Talmage and Jaromir stopped and looked behind them. Staring at the arch stone door standing in the darkness, the twin brothers gripped each other around the shoulders and left the dead behind.

ABOUT THE AUTHOR

DOUGLAS W. T. SMITH is an Australian Fantasy Author.

In 2020, he had an episode published from his debut novel, 'TO WIELD THE STARS', in the 'Of Metal and Magic CORE Collection: Year One Compendium'. His short stories have been published in a variety of magazines such as Movement, SuckerCo, Tertangala, and Needle in the Hay. Smith was shortlisted in the 2015 Historical Faction Award and the 2015 Science Fiction Award.

Between writing and reading fantasy stories, Smith embarks on his own adventures in nature with his wife, son, and dog. When indoors, Smith shares his writing journey on his blog and scribes insightful writing advice as the official Content Developer for the Of Metal and Magic Publishing website.

www.dwtsmith.com

.

Printed in Great Britain
by Amazon

63403208R00068